spyhole
secrets

Also by Zilpha Keatley Snyder

FEATURING THE STANLEY FAMILY
THE HEADLESS CUPID
THE FAMOUS STANLEY KIDNAPPING CASE
BLAIR'S NIGHTMARE
JANIE'S PRIVATE EYES

AND CONDORS DANCED
BLACK AND BLUE MAGIC
CAT RUNNING
THE CHANGELING
THE EGYPT GAME
FOOL'S GOLD
GIB AND THE GRAY GHOST
GIB RIDES HOME
THE GYPSY GAME
LIBBY ON WEDNESDAY
THE RUNAWAYS
SEASON OF PONIES
SONG OF THE GARGOYLE
SQUEAK SAVES THE DAY
THE TRESPASSERS
THE TRUTH ABOUT STONE HOLLOW
THE VELVET ROOM
THE WITCHES OF WORM

spyhole secrets

ZILPHA KEATLEY SNYDER

DELACORTE PRESS

Published by
Delacorte Press
an imprint of
Random House Children's Books
a division of Random House, Inc.
1540 Broadway
New York, New York 10036

Visit us on the Web! www.randomhouse.com/kids
Educators and librarians, for a variety of teaching tools, visit us at
www.randomhouse.com/teachers

Library of Congress Cataloging-in-Publication Data
Snyder, Zilpha Keatley.
    Spyhole Secrets / Zilpha Keatley Snyder.
        p. cm.
    Summary: When Hallie and her mother move to a new town after her father's sudden death, Hallie begins to spy on a troubled family living in a nearby building and her involvement helps her begin to handle her feelings of anger and grief.
    ISBN 0-385-32764-1 (trade)—ISBN 0-385-90016-3 (lib. bdg.)
    [1. Grief—Fiction. 2. Death—Fiction. 3. Family problems—Fiction.]
    I. Title.
    PZ7.S68522 Sp 2001
    [Fic]—dc21

                                                                00-048508

The text of this book is set in 13-point Legacy Serif.

Book design by Melissa Knight

Manufactured in the United States of America

June 2001

10 9 8 7 6 5 4 3 2 1

BVG

◎

*To the little girl I saw on television whose life
had just been tragically transformed by a tornado,
and whose grief and anger inspired Hallie's story*

When that long, weird day was finally over, Hallie went to bed without telling anyone about the attic window. Not her mother, and certainly not the second-floor Tilsons. Not even Marty, but for an entirely different reason.

She couldn't tell her mother or Mrs. Tilson because they both knew that the attic was forbidden territory. But why not call up Marty and tell her? The only answer had to be that Marty couldn't handle it. Hard to believe, but there it was. Not even Marty Goldberg, who'd been Hallie's best friend for nearly six years, and who used to go along with some fairly far-out fantasy stuff, could be expected to buy this one. How could anyone really believe that Hallie Meredith had found a secret window that let her spy on other people's lives without the slightest chance that anyone would know she was doing it?

Sound impossible? And if not impossible, something like black magic? Or else a miracle? You might think so, but it wasn't any of those things. Not really.

First off, it wasn't a miracle sent by God, that was for sure. As far as Hallie could tell, God had stopped paying attention to anything that happened to the Merediths a long time ago. And supernatural? No way. Magic stuff doesn't just up and happen that way. Everybody knows that in movies or on TV the supernatural doesn't start without some mysterious clue that lets you know what to expect. Something like a swirling cloud of icy air drifting down a staircase, for instance, or maybe finding a strangely shaped Arabian lamp. Right? Or at the very least there has to be a sudden shift in the whole atmosphere, like in the movies when the music changes key and goes spooky and ominous.

In this case there wasn't anything like that. On that Tuesday afternoon Hallie certainly hadn't been looking for anything magical or even out of the ordinary. As a matter of fact, she hadn't been looking for, or even looking forward to, anything at all. Particularly not looking *forward to*. Not just then, and maybe not ever again. What she *had* been doing was—well, a little bit like hiding.

Quite a lot like hiding, really, but not the sort you do for fun, as in a game of hide-and-seek. And not exactly the kind you do when you're trying to get away from somebody. Not unless the somebody is your own miserable self.

Now, *that* was getting close. What she'd really been looking for at that moment was a hiding place good enough to get her away from all the horrible stuff that had been happening in her life lately. And—in particular—to get away from the unbelievably dumb lie she had just told.

Actually, the first few hours of that weird Tuesday hadn't been any worse than the Monday that came before it, at least not until school was out. During the school day most of her new classmates at Irvington Middle School had been nice enough to simply ignore her. There had been a few, however, who'd gone out of their way to make it absolutely clear that anybody who hadn't had the privilege of knowing them since kindergarten was certain to be a hopeless bore. But that wasn't anything new. They'd already let her know how they felt about that the day before. It was what had happened *after* school on Tuesday that was especially disgusting. And the worst part of it was that it had been her own fault.

It had been Hallie's fault, all right, but another kid had actually started the whole thing. The only kid, strangely enough, who hadn't gone along with the class's "Let's make the new kid feel like an idiot" routine. Her name was Erin and she was blondish and kind of bulgy and embarrassingly enthusiastic about everything. But she was someone to talk to during recesses and lunch. Or at least to listen to.

Erin was a babbler. The kind of person Dad would

have said tended to say a lot of things she hadn't thought of yet. Hallie had listened to Erin's silly babbling on everything under the sun, including an endless rave about how she, Erin Adelaide Barlow, had lived in Irvington all her life, and how she knew practically everybody in town, and how much she liked meeting new people.

During lunch hour that Tuesday, the topic had been the important people in Irvington who were on the city council, and how important the city council was, and how Erin's very own mother was on it. Which was just before she asked the question that caused the problem.

Erin didn't ask many questions. Most of the time she was too busy answering questions that hadn't been asked. But she had gotten around to asking where Hallie's parents worked and what they did. So Hallie mentioned her mother's job at the savings and loan. That turned out to be just about the only thing she had a chance to say, which was great. She hadn't been planning to mention her father at all. And she didn't, at least not until she told the stupid lie.

Hallie had tried to be interested in Erin's conversation, and to be glad that at least one of her new classmates wanted to be friendly, but the truth of the matter was that she hadn't been all that grateful. And she'd been even less grateful when Erin caught up with her on the sidewalk right after school was out.

"Where is it you said you lived?" Erin asked. When

she heard "Warwick Avenue," she said, "Oh, good. I can go home that way. It's only a little bit out of my way."

So then, of course, they'd wound up in front of the Warwick Mansion and Erin had gone into a stark raving seizure about it. About how she'd always adored the old Warwick Mansion and how it had been her favorite Victorian house practically *forever*.

"And you actually live there?" she kept saying. "I can't believe it." Erin's whisper couldn't have sounded any more stoked if she'd been talking about Bluebeard's castle. "I just love that huge tower with all those stained-glass windows and gingerbready trim. It really is like a palace, isn't it? My mother says it used to be the most famous house in the whole city. She was so angry when the city let them divide it up into apartments and then..." She stopped to glare up at the ten-story building next door. "And then, worst of all, let them build that ugly high-rise practically touching it."

She stopped staring at the Warwick Towers high-rise long enough to grab Hallie's hand and squeeze it. "I just can't believe I'm lucky enough to meet someone who actually lives there." Erin's plump cheeks were positively quivering with enthusiasm. "Can I go in with you, Hallie? Can I?" And then, when she noticed the look on Hallie's face, "Just for a minute, to see what it looks like inside. I won't stay long."

That was when Hallie told the unbelievably crazy

lie. Crazy because Erin was certain to learn the truth—if she didn't already know it. And unbelievable because Hallie had no idea why she'd stammered out that she couldn't have visitors just then because . . . "Because my father works nights, so he has to sleep during the day. He's probably sleeping right now." That was what she'd actually said. *Her father worked nights! Her father, Alexander Meredith, who just happened to be dead, and had been for almost three months.*

Hallie was still talking and, at the same time, wondering why on earth she was saying such a ridiculous thing, when she realized that Erin was staring at her. Staring at her as if—well, as if maybe she had already heard that the new girl's father was dead. And probably had only asked about Hallie's parents to see if she could get her to talk about the terrible freeway accident. And now she must be wondering if Hallie was flipping out, or was a compulsive liar, or what. She didn't say so, of course. All Erin said was "Well, okay. Maybe some other time."

She left then, hurrying up Warwick Avenue as if she couldn't wait to get away from a person who would tell such a crazy, pointless lie. Hallie watched her go, feeling more or less the same way—feeling a sudden need to get away to a place where she could curl up like a bug in a cocoon and forget everything about Hallie Meredith. Forget her whole messed-up life, and especially the stupid lie she'd just told.

But in spite of the urge to run and hide, Hallie

went on standing there for several seconds while her mind began to spin out reasons and excuses, none of which made any more sense than the lie itself. Reasons like it had only happened because of how much she hated letting anybody, not just Erin but *anybody*, see where she lived. Actually, there wasn't anything crazy about that. Anyone who grew up living in a house like the one in Bloomfield, and then had to move into a really crummy apartment, would feel the same way.

So that was what started it. She'd suddenly needed to think up an excuse to keep Erin from coming in, and the first thing that popped into her mind had been to say that her mother worked nights and slept during the day. But then, with her mouth open to speak, she'd remembered that she'd already told Erin about the Irvington Savings and Loan. So there went that good idea. Erin Barlow might not be a giant brain, but she was probably smart enough to know that savings and loans didn't have night shifts. So the working nights story had to be changed in a big hurry. And that explained the stupid lie—or did it? Hallie hoped so, since the only other possibility was that she really was as crazy as Erin probably thought she was.

2

It wasn't until Erin had disappeared up Warwick Avenue that Hallie went on into the house. In through the grand double doors to the wide entry hall with its majestic spiral staircase which, except for some scruffy old rugs and peeling paint, probably looked almost as glorious as Erin had been expecting it to be.

On the second floor a wide, well-lit hallway passed the doors to the fairly nice apartments. But then came a climb up the steep and narrow back stairs, the air getting thinner and the heat heavier with every step. At last, puffing and sweating, she reached a small enclosed landing where the only light came from a tiny window, and where there were only two doors. Both were closed and locked—like the forbidden doors at the top of Bluebeard's castle.

One of the doors actually did lead to forbidden territory, but the one on the right was—home. The

Merediths' home sweet home, or else the Merediths' cell block, which was a much better name for it.

Taking out her key, Hallie opened the door, closed it behind her, and walked down a hallway past a row of cell-like rooms that had once been the Warwicks' servants' quarters. Five incredibly tiny, dark rooms strung out along a narrow hall that, since August, had been the home of the Meredith family from Bloomfield. Hallie clenched her teeth and swallowed hard. All that was left of the Meredith family, at least.

It was then, as she was hurrying down the hall to the kitchen to dump her books on the table, that Hallie really began to think about hiding. No, not think, actually. *Think* wasn't the right word. It wasn't the kind of thing you really thought about. It was more like something that you just let happen.

Actually, she'd always liked having a secret hiding place, even back in Bloomfield when it had been a kind of game. She'd never understood why exactly, but when she was curled up in the crotch of the old peach tree or under the desk in her dad's study, it had always seemed easier to have a conversation with God if she felt like it, or just to daydream and think her own private thoughts.

Back then she could always call up a wonderful fantasy about the great things that might happen someday. Like the one about the animal talent scout who discovered what an incredibly smart dog Zeus was and gave him his own TV series. The kind of stupid, "don't you wish" daydreams most normal kids have.

But all that had been in beautiful Bloomfield before the tenth of June. Now it was September, and the place was a crummy apartment on the third floor of what had once been the private home of a rich family. A very rich, very dead family named Warwick. And daydreams were definitely out of the picture. Hallie was quite sure she would never daydream again, and as for talking to God, no more of that either.

The hiding thing had gone through a lot of changes too. The way it had been happening lately was that one minute she would be sitting in front of the TV or at the kitchen table, and the next she'd be squeezed into the back of her tiny closet or curled up on a blanket behind the couch. The hiding places had changed a lot, but the biggest change was that none of it felt much like a game anymore.

This time, on a weird Tuesday afternoon, Hallie had no more than walked in the door of the ratty old cell block when she found herself drifting toward her tiny bedroom with its even tinier closet. And then, when she was almost there, stopping and turning around in a slow circle before she headed in an entirely different direction.

In a different direction and toward a different kind of hiding place. This time she was headed—for a moment she hardly knew where. . . . It wasn't until she got to the kitchen that she knew for certain: She was going to the attic. The attic of the Warwick Mansion, a place she had been only once before, and which, according to Mrs. Crowley, she was never to visit again unless "accompanied by a responsible adult."

That first attic visit had happened almost a month before, when she and her mother were moving into what Hallie had already started thinking of as the cell block. They'd been standing in the middle of their tiny living room surrounded by dozens of unpacked boxes when Mrs. Crowley, the apartment manager, had dropped in for a visit. Actually, she'd only come to have Hallie's mom sign some lease papers, and it wasn't until she was about to leave that she told them about the storage space in the attic. And *that* wasn't until after they'd listened to a little lecture about what kind of people shouldn't expect too much out of life.

The apartment manager hadn't exactly said she was talking about a single parent and her kid, but that was obviously what she had in mind. The main part of the message turned out to be that one of the things such people shouldn't expect out of life was an apartment with decent closet space, not to mention air-conditioning.

Mrs. Crowley was smiling a wide, toothy smile when she lumped Hallie and Paula Meredith together with all the rest of the people in the world who expected too much. The smile didn't make what she was saying any friendlier, however. In fact, Mrs. Crowley had the kind of smile that somehow managed to make almost anything she said come out the opposite of warm and friendly. Hallie remembered how her dad had described a smile like that as looking like a row of tombstones in January. Remembering how her father's eyes could laugh even while his mouth didn't had made a swelling at the back of Hallie's throat, but she'd swallowed it away and went on pretending to listen to the lecture.

After her little speech, Mrs. Crowley did come through with a key to the attic, but when she'd realized that Hallie was going to help carry up the boxes she'd added pointedly that *unaccompanied* children were *never* allowed in the attic. Hallie wanted to point out that a person who'd lived almost twelve years and had already been through some pretty terrible stuff wasn't exactly a child. But she didn't say it. Instead she bit her lip and went on biting it while Mrs. Crowley went on to hint that *the attic was haunted.*

She didn't come right out and say there were ghosts in the attic. What Mrs. Crowley actually said was something like "There's plenty of empty storage space up there. But most of the other tenants prefer to keep their extra belongings elsewhere. Not sure why exactly. Something to do with the rumors, I guess." And when Hallie's mother had asked, "What rumors?" she'd only muttered something about how there was always silly talk about old houses. She had still been smiling her tombstone smile as she'd added, "All nonsense, of course. No such thing as ghosts."

Remembering Mrs. Crowley's warning, Hallie shrugged. She didn't believe that haunted stuff. Not for a minute. Mrs. Crowley had probably made that ghostly rumors stuff up to make sure Hallie never did exactly what she was, at that very minute, getting ready to do. And what if the attic did turn out to be haunted? Big deal. Maybe a really scary ghost or two would be enough to take her mind off some other terrible stuff, at least for a while.

According to the wall clock over the old-fashioned refrigerator, there was still plenty of time. Not quite three-thirty. More than an hour before her mother came home from work. And the key? The key that Mrs. Crowley had put on the shelf over the kitchen sink? Still there. Good. Smiling grimly, Hallie whispered, "Look out, ghosts, here I come."

She was hurrying now, wanting to get going before her conscience had time to tell her all the reasons she shouldn't do it. Not that she'd listen if it did. Oh, sure, she used to believe there had to be good reasons for everything that happened in this world. Used to, but not anymore. So her conscience could just shut up and mind its own business.

With the key to the attic in her pocket, Hallie headed for the door. But then, just before she went out into the stairwell, she did stop for a second or two. Stopped to think, the way her mother's bossy friend, Ellen, was always urging her to do.

"Think before you jump, Hallie," Ellen was always saying. "You're entirely too impulsive." But this time it didn't work the way Ellen was always hoping it would. Actually, all that particular moment of thought led to was the realization that she ought to get a move on while she still had the time. A minute later, Hallie unlocked the attic door and started up the stairs.

3

At the top of the narrow attic stairs, Hallie stopped for a minute, but it was only to let her eyes adjust to the lack of light. She stopped once again a few steps farther on, so the rest of her could adjust to the attic itself. It seemed, somehow, quite different from when she'd been there with her mother. Almost as if she'd never been there before.

It was hotter, for one thing, and dustier. It had been a very warm day, and the sun beating down on the sloping roof had turned the attic into a stifling oven. When she breathed deeply, she could feel the heat burning its way down into her lungs. The long, narrow space with its slanting, cross-beamed ceiling seemed larger, and the light—what there was of it— was dim and shadow-haunted. Seeping through the colored-glass panes of the small dormer windows, its rays stained the rough wood floor with blurry splotches of blue, red, and green.

The silence was different too, so deep she could

almost feel it, like a thick, enveloping wall. She stood still, listening and breathing hard. At last she shrugged away a shiver and moved on.

Not far from the stairwell she came to a familiar stack of heavily taped boxes. Boxes she recognized as the ones she'd helped pack with things like her mother's art supplies and her fancy china that had been used only when company came. Hallie shrugged. The oil paints and the china might as well be stored away; it wasn't as if they'd be using them much here in Irvington. Her mother wouldn't have time to do much painting anymore now that she had to work full time. And the friends who used to come to dinner all lived a long way from Irvington.

Hallie was still reading the labels on the storage boxes when she came to one that really got to her. Her fists clenched and she felt her face flush with anger as she read the label. In big capital letters it said SLEEPING BASKET and LITTER BOX. There they were, wrapped up and hidden in a forgotten attic when they shouldn't have had to be stored away at all—and wouldn't have been, if it weren't for that very first rule on the Warwick lease papers. The most important rule, according to Mrs. Crowley. The one that said NO PETS (in capital letters).

As Hallie moved on, she passed a couple of other smallish collections of crates and boxes, no doubt the belongings of other Warwick tenants. But nothing more, except for a procession of wide brick chimney flues. The rest of the long stretch of shadowy space seemed to be entirely empty—empty and silent. No moans or sighs, not even any drifting white mists or patches of icy air.

Curling up one side of her mouth, the way her father always did when someone was being particularly ridiculous, Hallie tried to make her voice sound like his as she whispered, "What's this, Mrs. Tombstone? Don't tell me your ghost friends are out to lunch."

"Yeah, out to lunch," she agreed in her own voice. She was almost disappointed. As a ghost hangout, the Warwick attic left a lot to the imagination. There at least ought to be a few mysterious-looking objects lying around. Like a puppet with a sinister face. Or perhaps a huge antique desk that might have a secret drawer or two. As a matter of fact, in the whole poor excuse for a haunted attic there wasn't anything a ghost, or a person, might hide behind. Or even sit down on comfortably.

She was walking past another stack of boxes when she became aware of a circular alcove in the farthest corner of the room. Another tower room. Of course there would be one in the attic, just as there was on each of the other floors. In fact, now that she thought of it, she remembered noticing the attic's tower room from the sidewalk below. Remembered looking way up to where the tower's highest level tapered to a cone-shaped roof topped by a thin, pointed spire.

As she cautiously moved toward it through deepening shadows, Hallie wondered why the light was so dim. The other tower rooms had circular windowpanes, with colored-glass panels at eye level and clear glass up above. The one in the Tilsons' second-floor apartment also had curving built-in seats. But this one seemed to have no windows and no window seats. Nothing much to sit on or hide behind, except for a dim shape that turned out to be a small metal trunk.

When Hallie walked into the deeply shadowed tower room, it wasn't because she was thinking of it as a possible hiding place. The metal trunk just happened to be the best place, practically the only place, to sit down. And as for the window, she hadn't even noticed there was one. Not yet.

It wasn't until she'd been sitting on the trunk for a minute or two that Hallie began to really think about the lack of windows. The windows in the Tilsons' second-floor apartment, for instance, had large flower-shaped stained-glass panes that looked directly into the shops and offices on the lower floors of the building next door. There were greens that turned the people in the shops and offices across the air well into a bunch of green-skinned extraterrestrial creatures. Even on the third floor, where the tower alcove made up most of the Merediths' tiny living room, there was a small circular window of stained glass that looked out into an architect's studio.

But here in the attic's tower room there seemed, at first, to be no windows at all. Yet as she sat on the old trunk, Hallie became aware of a strip of bluish light that oozed out of a slit in the tower wall.

So there had been windows after all, but they'd been covered over with . . . Reaching out, she touched what seemed to be a thin panel of rough wood or plasterboard. Something had been nailed over the entire window area, except for that one place where a small slice of paneling had fallen away, allowing a band of light to shine through. Blue light. Forgetting the heat, the stifling air, and even Mrs. Crowley's ghosts, Hallie leaned forward.

It wasn't until her cheek was almost touching the paneling that she was able to see. Out through wavy blue glass, across a very narrow air well, and right into some other people's lives.

4

The window on the other side of the air well was large and uncurtained, and the room beyond it was long and narrow. And all of it, everything Hallie could see, appeared to be swimming in ripples of blue light. It took her a moment to realize that the color didn't come from the room itself, but from the stained glass in her spyhole. And another few seconds to realize that the wavy underwater look probably came from the imperfections in the old glass. By moving her head up and down, she could set off waves of blue light that turned the room into a scene from a mermaid movie, or maybe an underwater lounge for scuba divers.

Except for the blue light, however, the room she was looking into seemed strangely uninteresting. There was a large, heavy blob-shaped couch with a matching love seat at one end of the room, and at the other, a dining table and chairs. But other than a stack of newspapers on one of the couches and a coat or jacket draped over the back of a chair, nothing even hinted at living occupants. There were no pictures on the walls, no vases or candles, nothing the least bit decorative sitting around on shelves or sideboards. The whole scene, Hallie decided, was more like a furniture store arrangement than a home where real people lived.

She wrinkled her nose. Having been raised by an artistic mother and a father who liked his surroundings to be lively and original, she couldn't help wondering what kind of people would live in such a dull, impersonal environment. There was nothing interesting about any of it, except, of course, for the strange blue light. That and the fact that she was able to observe the whole scene without being seen, like a magical, four-stories-tall Peeping Tom.

She was beginning to understand why this window had been covered over. The tower rooms on the lower levels were just as close to the new building, but their windows only looked into public places like stores and offices. But up here, where the high-rise apartments began, no one would want a neighboring window so close to the big picture window in their fourth-floor apartment. It was an easy guess that the apartment owner had complained and the window had been boarded up. So their privacy problem had been solved, or so they thought.

Hallie leaned over again to peer through the slit in the paneling and the pane of blue glass. This time, on closer inspection, she did notice one interesting object in the living room area. It was sitting high up on the mantel over the fireplace, and it appeared to be some kind of mask. A very large mask with a feathery headdress, big bushy eyebrows, and a wide, crooked mouth full of jagged teeth. But even that, and the fact that it was there, had an accidental feel to it, as if it had been left there by mistake.

Hallie was still staring at the mask when she suddenly realized that someone was in the room. She hadn't noticed a door opening, but then, without any warning, someone was walking across the room. It was a woman—no, a girl, a teenager maybe, not much older than Hallie herself.

The first thing she noticed about the girl, the one thing no one could help noticing, was her hair. A pale blond streaked with darker shades of gold, it hung straight down below her waist. She was wearing a white T-shirt and a long denim jumper, but mostly what she seemed to be wearing was a thick, sleek shawl of shimmering hair.

She came slowly across the room with her lips and eyebrows scrunched into what seemed to be a frown. She looked angry, or sad, or maybe a little of both. Stopping once to look around, she dropped a backpack on the dining room table and came directly toward the window. Right to the window that opened on the air well, so close that for a moment Hallie ducked away, certain she would be seen. But when she cautiously put her eye back to the opening, the girl was still looking away from her, out the window and down toward Warwick Avenue.

She had an unusual face, Hallie thought. Not just cute in the ordinary teenage girl way, with a pug nose and lots of eyelashes. And not the kind of face you can describe the best features of, like sexy eyes or movie-star lips. But the whole face, eyes and nose and mouth, was put together in an interesting way so that it somehow resembled a face from an old painting, or maybe from a fairy tale or an ancient myth.

But it was mostly the hair that was so extraordinary. Long, straight, and heavy, its blondness tinged to a greenish shimmer by the blue light, it looked like the hair of some kind of supernatural being. A mermaid, maybe. Or that princess who let her hair down from the tower so her boyfriend, the prince, could use it as a ladder. Rapunzel, that was it. It definitely did look like the hair of a Rapunzel-type fairy-tale princess.

The Rapunzel girl stayed at the window for a long time and, across the air well, so did Hallie, even though she definitely felt uncomfortable about what she was doing. At first only physically uncomfortable, from the sweltering heat, but as time passed there was another kind of discomfort that got stronger the longer she went on watching. She didn't know why exactly, except that staring right into the face of someone who didn't know you were there was definitely a weird sensation. Kind of nightmarish, actually, almost like being invisible.

Several long, fascinating but uneasy minutes passed before the girl suddenly turned away, went to where she'd left her backpack, and then came back, holding a piece of paper in both hands. Back at the window, she went on looking first at the paper and then out toward Warwick Avenue while her expression changed and changed again, from quivering-lip tragic to happy anticipation—and back to tragic. And Hallie went on watching her and wondering who she was and what she was doing and why.

At last the girl shook her head hard, flipped a long sheaf of hair back over her shoulder, turned slowly away, and left the room.

Nothing more happened. Nothing moved in the blue-lit room except when Hallie moved her head enough to set waves of blue light rippling across the striped wallpaper and klutzy furniture. But she stayed at the spyhole until her watch reminded her that it was time to leave. Her mother would be home soon.

Making her way back across the attic, Hallie thought about the girl with the Rapunzel hair even while she was keeping one eye out for Mrs. Crowley's ghosts. Other frustrating things were crowding back into her mind, like the snobby kids at Irvington Middle School and the unbelievable lie she'd just told

Erin. But the Rapunzel girl and the secret spyhole were there too, at least until she was in her own apartment again.

By five o'clock, however, everything was back to normal. At least back to what had been more or less normal lately, which meant that by the time her mother came home, Hallie was curled up in the old leather chair that had been her dad's, with her eyes closed and an unopened book in her lap.

Paula Meredith put a bag of groceries away in the kitchen before she stuck her head around the corner and said, "There you are, sweetie. So, how was school today? Better than yesterday, I hope."

Hallie opened her eyes and shrugged and, in a tone of voice that made it mean just the opposite, said, "School? Oh, great. Absolutely fabulous."

"Oh? Absolutely fabulous, huh?" Her mother knew she didn't mean it. Her savings-and-loan smile, the kind she put on every day like a uniform, faded a little. Hallie was glad to see it go. She hated it when her mother's cheerfulness obviously said "See how brave I'm being, and it's all for your sake."

Hallie sighed and looked away, hiding her eyes. She hated her mother's phony smiles, but . . . She shrugged and shook her head, trying not to remember that she hated it even more when it felt as if the smiles were starting to be real. As if maybe her mother already was starting to forgive God for what had happened to the Merediths only three months before, on that awful tenth day of June.

Hallie's anger flared up again and then soured into a feeling of guilt. Guilt for wanting her mother to go on feeling the way they both did that day when the policeman came to the door to ask Hallie's mother if she was Mrs. Meredith. To ask that one question and then to say "I'm afraid I have bad news, Mrs. Meredith."

"Yeah, fabulous," Hallie said again, trying this time to sound as if she really meant it. Then she clenched her teeth, shut her eyes, and kept them shut until her mother went back into the kitchen.

Dinner that night was, as usual, mostly microwave stuff. Hallie didn't blame her mother for that, at least not very much. She could remember how she and her father used to kid her mother about being a gourmet cook, or at least a very adventuresome one, always trying out new recipes. But that was another thing that had changed a lot since Bloomfield. Oh, it was probably true, as her mother kept reminding her, that it was hard to switch over to recipe books when you've been reading financial statements all day. Still, microwave lasagna for the third time in a week and grocery-store cookies for dessert didn't do a whole lot to improve a less-than-perfect day. Even though she was pretty hungry, Hallie hardly ate anything.

The cookies were still waiting on the table and

Hallie's mind was wandering when her mother reached over to pat her on the arm. "Hallie," she said, "did you hear me? You seem to be a million miles away."

"Hear you? Oh, I guess not." Hallie shook her head. "Was it something about . . ." A word or two floated back. "Was it something about the Tilsons?"

Her mother sighed and shook her head. "What I said was, I forgot to drop off the Tilsons' yogurt. Could you run it down for me?"

The Tilsons, who lived in one of the halfway-nice apartments on the second floor, were always having her mother pick up things for them at the store. Especially yogurt. The Tilsons ate a lot of yogurt.

"Not again," Hallie said. Getting the big carton out of the refrigerator, she reluctantly started downstairs. Reluctantly because the Tilsons were too . . . *Yeah, too what?* Hallie asked herself. The Tilsons were a really old couple who had been superhelpful when the Merediths arrived at the Warwick Mansion, clueing them in on important information like where to pick up their mail and how to keep the ancient coin-operated washing machine from flooding the whole basement. They'd even gone so far as to send up some cherry pie on that first day. And not just two pieces—a whole freshly baked cherry pie.

So they were too what? Too friendly? Or maybe too sympathetic? Or too nosy? Yeah, that was it. The

Tilsons were too nosy, Hallie decided as she rang their doorbell.

"Well, Hallie, my girl," Mr. Tilson said as he opened the door and peered out, "how good to see you again." Under his close-cropped white hair his small, sharp eyes positively glowed with curiosity. "Do come in."

"Yes, yes." His wife, whose name was Annette, was right behind him. "So good to see you. We've been wondering about how you're getting along now that school has started." Her eyes had the same super-snoopy glow. The Tilsons, who'd been married practically forever, looked a lot alike—small, pale, and furry, like the same kind of little animal. Rabbits, maybe, but with small round ears instead of big floppy ones. Two small, round-eared, nosy rabbits.

Hallie said hello, and as she quickly handed over the carton, she managed to change the subject from Irvington Middle School to yogurt and whether her mother had remembered to buy the right flavor. She had. It figured; Paula Meredith usually didn't make that kind of mistake. And then Mrs. Tilson was saying, "Hallie dear. We were about to have a piece of cherry pie. Wouldn't you like to join us?"

Hallie wouldn't like to. At least she wouldn't have, if it hadn't been for the pie. But she remembered Annette Tilson's cherry pie, or at least her taste buds certainly did. So much so that she had to swallow quickly before she said, "Hey great." She swallowed again and added, "But I can't stay long. Homework, you know."

At the Tilsons' kitchen table there were thick slabs of luscious pie, cups of tea for the Tilsons, and a glass of milk for Hallie. And, just as she'd feared, a lot of nosy questions. The questions and comments about her school were bad enough. Questions like "Are you finding your classes interesting?"

"Yeah." Hallie shrugged. "Some of them." But what she wanted to say was, *Yeah, really interesting, if you don't mind being around a lot of people who hate you and make sure you know it.*

And then "I suppose you're making lots of new friends?" *Yeah, really good friends. The kind who just act like they think you're already dead, instead of actually trying to kill you.*

But the questions about her mother were the worst. After a lot of comments about what a lovely lady Paula Meredith was and how she reminded them of their own dear daughter who lived far away in Massachusetts, Mrs. Tilson said, "We've been worrying about your mother, dear. She's been looking so tired lately. Working such long hours and with all the household duties to handle by herself. I hope you're doing all you can to help."

That did it. The throat-swelling, eye-burning rage flared up like an erupting volcano.

"Yeah, I try to help her." Hallie pushed away her pie plate and got to her feet. The Tilsons were staring up at her, looking more than ever like a pair of nervous rabbits. "At least I don't send her to the store all the time to buy yogurt for me."

She was heading for the door when the guilt thing kicked in, mixing up the hard, clean anger and turning it into a miserable, stomach-tightening confusion. She turned back long enough to mumble, "Thanks for the pie," and then, halfway out the door and halfway crying, she stopped again, this time to choke out, "I'm sorry." Then she ran down the hall and up the stairs to the third floor. She was still running and crying when she got back home.

5

Outside the door to the cell block, Hallie wiped her eyes and clenched her teeth, biting off the urge to sob. It didn't take long. She'd had a lot of practice at that sort of thing lately. At swallowing sobs and wiping pain and anger off her face. She waited until she thought everything was under control before she went on in.

On her way to her bedroom she stuck her head through the kitchen door and said, "They said to tell you thanks for the yogurt." She swallowed hard to clear her throat before she went on, "I had some cherry pie."

Still at the kitchen sink, her mother turned her head, "Oh, good for you," she said. "Annette's cherry pie is just about..." But by then Hallie was out of earshot, on her way to her bedroom. Closing the door firmly behind her, she sat down on the bed, then got up again to look in the small oval mirror over her dresser. Leaning forward until her face filled the mirror, she checked out her eyes first—red and puffy, and angry too. And not just her eyes. Her whole face looked tight and ugly with anger. Positively ugly.

Feeling shocked, she reached up to wipe her eyes and run her fingers across her cheeks. Forcing her lips into a phony smile, she tried to remind herself how she used to look. Pretty, people used to say. What a pretty girl, and such a charming one-dimple smile. She smiled a phony, charming smile again and held it until the tears came back. She watched a tear run over the spot where the dimple had been before she flopped down to bury her face in the pillow.

Lying there, facedown, she reached back for the anger, asking herself, "What gives those people the right to stick their noses into our business? Or the right to tell me what to do?" It worked for a little while.

One of the things she'd learned since June was that being really mad could crowd out worse stuff. Not always, and not for very long, but quite often anger was better than tears. She'd learned a lot about such things since the Monday morning when her father had started for work a little early on the day of the chain-reaction pileup on the foggy freeway.

She'd been angry a lot since that day. Angry at God for the fog and for letting her father be one of the drivers who got caught in it. And angry at her mother for fussing at Dad to start early that morning so he wouldn't have to drive so fast.

"I worry about you trying to hurry on that crowded freeway," her mother had said. "Why don't you try starting a little earlier?" And so he had. Just early enough to be caught in one of the worst freeway disasters that had ever happened.

Not that she held that against her mother, at least not very much. After all, her mother hadn't meant it to turn out the way it did. But there were other things. Things like what she'd said when Hallie complained about having to sell their house. Things about some bad investments Dad had made, as if losing their house had been all his fault. And there had been plenty of other things to be angry about.

She'd hated it when her mother couldn't find a job anywhere near Bloomfield and had to start looking in places like Irvington. And she'd hated it even more when it turned out they had to move into Warwick Mansion, just because it was cheap and close to her mother's new job. Into a tiny, ugly—not to mention hot and airless—apartment.

But the worst thing about Warwick Mansion, of course, was rule number one on the lease contract that her mother had actually signed, even after Hallie had told her she'd rather be homeless than sign a thing like that. Rule number one, the no pets rule, which meant that both Zeus and Thisbe belonged to other people now.

The trouble with anger, though, as Mom's busybody friend, Ellen, was always saying, was that it didn't solve anything and it didn't last. No matter how hard you tried to hang on, it eventually faded away, leaving you with other feelings that were even worse. "Like guilt, for instance," Ellen liked to say. "Like guilt for the things you said or did while you were too angry to think straight."

"Well, forget that one," Hallie remembered telling Ellen. "Forget that guilt thing. Why should I feel guilty?"

The sound of footsteps interrupted her thoughts. Unclenching her jaw and fists, Hallie sat up and rubbed her face hard with both hands. She was sitting cross-legged, leafing through her language arts book, when her mother came in and asked how it was going.

"All right, I guess," Hallie said. "I just have to read this chapter and answer some questions about it."

"Could I see?" Her mother sat down at the foot of the bed, took the book, and holding Hallie's place with one finger, flipped through a few pages. When she gave it back she said, "Looks interesting. A lot more interesting than the textbooks we used to have." She smiled at Hallie—and Hallie smiled back. A small smile, but one she almost meant.

See, Ellen, Hallie thought, *anger does help. Once it burns itself out, you do feel better, at least for a while.* But later, when her mother said, "Good night, then. Think I'll go to bed early. I'm awfully tired," suddenly it was back again. Anger at her mother for the tiredness in her face and voice. And at the Tilsons for making it seem that it was Hallie's fault. Anger at everyone and everything.

Shoving her homework out of the way, she flopped down on the bed and stayed there until the bathroom pipes stopped gurgling and the door to her mother's bedroom opened and closed. Then she got up, got her slippers out of the closet, and tiptoed down the hall to the kitchen, where a small flashlight was kept under the sink and the key to the attic lay on the shelf over the sink.

The attic at night wasn't a whole lot of fun. It was still hot, for one thing, and somehow seemed even more airless than it had during the day. Breathtakingly hot and dark, and more deeply silent than seemed possible or likely. Actually, it was pretty terrifying, or at least it could have been for someone who hadn't stopped caring what happened to her. At the top of the stairs, Hallie stopped long enough to remember that she didn't care anymore. To remind herself that she wouldn't care a bit if a whole parade of ghosts appeared, or even a black-cloaked Dracula with long, bloody fangs.

Still standing near the stairwell, reminding herself why she didn't care, she shined the flashlight from side to side and saw—nothing at all. Less than nothing. The heavy darkness seemed to close in on the narrow beam, leaving only a pale slice of murky light that quickly faded to empty blackness. Empty, and yet wasn't there something? A shape she could almost see, or maybe a sound she couldn't quite hear.

With the restless hush pressing ever closer, Hallie moved forward, her heart pounding and her breath coming in sharp, quick gasps. Once, she actually stopped and headed for the stairs. But then, gritting her teeth, she turned back again toward the tower alcove and the secret spyhole.

When she sat down on the old trunk and leaned forward, her heart was still pounding wildly, and it continued to thunder against her ribs as fear quickly changed to eager anticipation. Forgetting the scary darkness behind her, she put her eye to the narrow opening.

The view was even better after dark. With all the lights on in the blue-tinged room across from the spyhole, everything was as clear and distinct as a brightly lit stage ready for some actors to appear and start the first act of a play. A play that would have to be about people who lived in an incredibly ugly fourth-floor apartment full of boring gray-brown furniture and who, like as not, were pretty stuffy and boring themselves. Except, of course, for the girl with the great hair.

The mysterious girl staring sadly down toward Warwick Avenue had reminded Hallie of the Rapunzel princess. Hallie remembered most of the story. How the prince would come to the prison tower and call for Rapunzel to let down her long hair. But the ending? She wished she could remember how the story ended for the fairy-tale Rapunzel and, even more, she wished she knew more about the real-life, modern one. What was happening in her life, Hallie wondered, that made her look so mournfully out the window for such a long time? What or who was she expecting to see?

Hallie was staring into the blue-tinged room wondering about the Rapunzel girl when she suddenly noticed something moving. Someone was in the room after all, and must have been there the whole time. Right there all the time, seated, no doubt, just beyond the windowed wall, where only their feet and lower legs were visible from Hallie's point of view. Dull brown pant legs and dark shoes that blended into the drab colors of the room, so that they only became noticeable when they began to move.

It was a man, Hallie decided, and judging by the size of his shoes, a big one. Not a kid; not a teenage boy either. Not with those dressy black leather shoes. Who was he, then, and what was he to Rapunzel? Her father? Hallie was considering whether that was the answer when a door swung open and someone rushed into the room. And there she was, Rapunzel herself.

She was dressed differently now, in a kimono with long flowing sleeves. Most of her heavy curtain of hair was pulled back and tied behind her neck, but a few strands had escaped and fell around her face in silky streamers.

Hallie stared, mystified and entranced. In the kimono, the girl looked even more like a character from a fairy tale. Her eyes had changed too. Instead of sad and dreamy they now seemed wide and wild, darting here and there as if in fright or anger. Her lips were moving rapidly, as if she was talking fast, or perhaps even yelling. What was she saying? Hallie could only wish desperately for Superman ears, or for the ability to read lips.

Rapunzel stopped talking then, for only a moment, perhaps listening to something the person in the chair was saying. When she began to talk again, her lips moved just as furiously as before. Then she whirled and ran out of the room.

Hallie was still staring at the door that had slammed shut behind Rapunzel when it flew open again and she reappeared, dragging something, or someone, behind her. Dragging—a monster! A small monster, not nearly as big as Rapunzel herself, but incredibly evil-looking. It was entirely wrapped in a long black cape, so that the shape of its body was blurred and vague. But its head was . . . unbelievable.

Beneath a crest of bristling feathers the head was large, much too large for its small body. On one of its irregular surfaces, a strange collection of features were jumbled together into what looked almost like a face: a long pointed nose, huge bushy eyebrows, and a grinning mouth full of long, sharp teeth. Almost a face, but not quite.

Pressing her eye to the spyhole and her cheek against the rough paneling, Hallie almost forgot to breathe as the monster and Rapunzel struggled, staggering back and forth across the room. Holding it away from her at arm's length, she pulled it this way and that while it twisted and turned, striking out at her now and then with spider-thin black arms.

The battle had been going on for what seemed like a very long time before the person in the chair got to his feet and began to intervene. Now that he was visible, Hallie could see that he was indeed a man: a tall, gray-haired man with a lean, narrow head. As he stood up and stomped across the room, his angular face was contorted by anger. And he, like Rapunzel, was obviously yelling, his mouth working fast and furiously.

Putting one hand on Rapunzel's shoulder and the other on the back of the little monster, he moved forward, pushing them both ahead of him. Shoving, struggling, and striking out, the three of them crossed the room and disappeared through a door that seemed to lead to a hallway. The room was empty again. Nothing moved except the wavering blue light.

Several minutes passed, during which Hallie remained at the spyhole waiting to see more, and wanting—not just wanting, desperately needing—to know more about what she had just seen. But when the man returned at last he was alone, and he stayed only long enough to turn out the lights. The blue-lit room disappeared into darkness, and Hallie returned to the reality of the enclosing tower room and, beyond it, the empty darkness of the Warwick Mansion attic.

The return trip across the attic was at a faster pace than the arrival, which somehow made it more frightening. Terrifying, actually. Walking fast in the flashlight's narrow beam, then almost running, she felt she was trying to escape something that was right behind her. Right behind her, and coming closer with every step. Something ghostly white that drifted after her through the darkness, or perhaps a small, shapeless, black-robed form that bounced over the floor.

When she was finally back in her own bed, Hallie shut her eyes tightly and pulled the covers over her face.

6

So that was the end of the weird Tuesday. It was over, a new day would soon begin, and nobody would know about the strange things that had happened the day before. No one but Hallie herself. And for a whole lot of reasons, it was going to have to stay that way.

Except for the part about Erin and the lie, of course. Hallie cringed, pulling the blankets up farther over her head. The lie. Why had she lied to Erin? And if she had had to lie to keep Erin from seeing the cell block, why hadn't she picked something to lie about besides Dad?

Dad. Hallie rocked her head on the pillow with her eyes squeezed tightly shut. She wasn't going to cry. Not anymore. *Enough is enough,* she told herself. Enough was all through June and July and most of August, when the tears had gone on every night in bed and lots of other times too, whenever something reminded her of what had happened or of how things used to be.

And in the mornings too, after a night of good dreams in which Dad was still alive and everything was back the way it had been before. Dreams in which she and Dad were playing with Zeus in the backyard or just sitting together, Dad in his leather chair and Hallie on the fat armrest, while they talked about everything from shaggy dog jokes to very private things like the kinds of things you said when you were talking to God. And then the dream would end and the tears would begin.

There had been lots of tears, up until the time when Zeus and Thisbe had gone off to live with their new owners and nearly everything the Merediths owned had been sold or packed into boxes. That had been in August, and it was not long afterward that Hallie began to work at making anger take the place of tears.

It usually started with the *why* questions: Why did it have to happen? And why to Dad? Why had God let Alex Meredith die, when everyone always said what a good person he was, and at the same time all kinds of other people went on living, some of them really bad people . . .

It was beginning to work. The angry fire was starting somewhere in her chest and soon it would begin to burn its way to her face, drying up the tears. She knew how to reach out for it now, welcoming it, calling up all the familiar words and phrases. She was well into the process when something, some momentary memory, began to interfere. The crack widened then, enough to allow other vivid bits and pieces to slide through.

At first it was mostly questions about the Rapunzel girl. Who was she? What was her real name and how old was she? And was there any way to find out? For some strange reason Hallie found herself really wanting to know the answers.

Not that it mattered, she told herself. Why should a person with all sorts of problems of her own be curious about a teenage stranger? So what if she had awesome hair and apparently lived with a small, ugly monster?

But the questions kept coming back. Was Rapunzel still in school, and if so, where did she go? Probably to a high school. Hallie had seen lots of high school kids on Warwick Avenue, particularly around the video game store on the corner of Fifteenth Street. But she'd never seen Rapunzel there, she was sure of that. She would have remembered if she had. Especially the hair. Hair like that would be hard to forget.

And then there was the monster with a face like some kind of primitive mask.... Wait a minute. It wasn't until that instant that Hallie realized that she had seen the monster before—at least its head. It was the word *mask* that had done it. That word brought back a memory of the object that had been on the mantel in the living room the first time she had looked through the spyhole. She was sure there had been a mask there. She remembered thinking that it was the most interesting thing in the whole room. But had it been missing that evening? She didn't remember.

Hallie sat straight up in bed, and for a moment she actually considered going back up to the attic to see if the mask was still on the mantel. But the thought of the long trek across the dark attic was definitely discouraging. Besides, the lights in the spyhole room were probably still turned off.

No, she wouldn't go back tonight, but next time she'd remember to check on the mask. If there was a next time. And in the meantime she'd just forget about it. Or at least try to.

Back under the covers, Hallie closed her eyes again and tried to shut her mind to everything. Particularly to everything that had happened that day at school, and on the walk home with Erin, and in the attic's tower alcove.

But—was the mask she'd seen on the mantel the kind that could be worn? And if so, how? And whose body could have looked so small and shapeless under a black robe? Hallie was still wondering when her mind began to drift and cloud. And then light was streaming into the room and it was another day.

Another day and another six miserable hours

at Irvington Middle School to look forward to. Actually, the worst part was going to be facing Erin again. Meeting Erin and trying to figure out just how crazy she thought Hallie was—which depended on whether she knew that Hallie's father was dead.

She was on her way to her first-period class when the dreaded meeting with Erin finally took place. When it was over Hallie had to admit she still didn't know how much Erin knew. Erin had been friendly enough. Almost as friendly as she had been the day before, which would seem to mean that either she didn't mind having crazy friends, or she really hadn't heard about Hallie's father.

Had she or hadn't she? Of course, it was a question that Hallie couldn't ask. But there was another question that she could ask: a question about Rapunzel. During lunch hour when she was on her way to the cafeteria, Hallie had her chance. Slowing down so that Erin could catch up, she said, "Hey, Erin. Do you know a blond girl, a teenager probably, who lives near where I do?"

Erin fell into step beside Hallie, delighted, as usual, to be asked a question, any question. "I probably do," she said. "I know a lot of people in Irvington."

"Yeah, I know." Hallie remembered the long speech she'd heard on the subject of how many people Erin knew.

"What's her name?" Erin asked.

45

"That's just it. I don't know," Hallie said. "That's why I'm asking you. But she has this awesome blond hair. Long, clear down past her waist, straight, and kind of shimmery gre—blond, that is." As she pictured the blue-tinged blond hair, she'd almost said green.

"Green hair?" Erin looked puzzled.

"No, blond. I said *blond.*"

Erin's round forehead wrinkled thoughtfully. "No. I don't remember anyone like that," she said. "She must not go to Irvington High. I might not know her if she doesn't go to Irvie. Most of the teenagers I know go there." So Erin was no help.

When the school day was finally over and Hallie was on her way home, she was careful to check out every passerby on Warwick Avenue. Particularly the teenagers. But there was no one who even came close to looking like Rapunzel.

And the monster? She didn't bother to look for the monster, of course. Even if it was a real person who had been wearing the mask, there was no way she'd recognize him, or her, without it. On the other hand, if the thing she'd seen wrestling with Rapunzel actually was some kind of monster, it certainly wouldn't be allowed out on the street.

Back in the Merediths' apartment, Hallie dumped her books on the kitchen table and checked her watch. There was plenty of time. Taking the key off its ledge, she headed for the attic.

7

There it was, the long, narrow room, looking just as drab and bare as before. Except that now, as Hallie leaned forward to the spyhole, she immediately saw that there were people in the room too. Two—no, three of them, but not at all the ones she was expecting. Not Rapunzel, that is, or the weird little monster either. In fact, the only two she could see well were complete strangers.

One of the strangers was a man wearing a grayish business suit and a solemn, businesslike expression. The other was a woman. A slim, good-looking woman with a great hairdo—but she was not at all pleasant looking. There was anger in the tight lines of her sleek, stylish face and in the sudden movements of her arms and hands.

The third person in the room was sitting in the same half-hidden chair where the man had sat the night before. And like the night before, all Hallie could see of him were his feet and legs. As Hallie

47

watched the scene from her spyhole, it became obvious that the man in the suit was speaking to the person in the chair. Talking on and on as if he was giving some kind of lecture.

As Mr. Gray Business Suit went on talking, swinging his arms in broad, forceful gestures, the woman watched him, nodding sharply. She glanced quickly at the person in the chair, and then very quickly looked away.

The conversation, or lecture, by Business Suit had been going on for some time before the person in the chair got to his feet and became—the same tall, gray-haired man Hallie had seen the night before. The man who finally had gotten up from the chair, separated Rapunzel and the little monster, and pushed them out of the room. And now, as he stepped forward, it seemed for a moment that he might be getting ready to do the same sort of thing. Hallie couldn't see much of his face but his clenched fist and hunched shoulders definitely looked threatening, and for a moment the faces of the other two looked uneasy. Frightened even, as if they were expecting to be pushed, if not something worse.

It was easy to see that something very serious was happening in the room. Possibly something really terrible. As Hallie pressed her eye to the spyhole, she became so caught up in what she was watching she almost forgot to breathe. Where she was and what she was doing were completely forgotten. The only thoughts in her mind were about the people in the blue-lit room. Who were they, what was going on, and what might happen next? And what did all of it, what did any of it, have to do with Rapunzel?

Just as Hallie was thinking about Rapunzel the door opened and there she was, in the same doorway where she had appeared the first time Hallie had seen her. She was dressed a little differently this time, in a long skirt and shorter T-shirt, with a different collection of jewelry. But as before, the total effect was definitely the *in* look. The same combination of expensive junk jewelry that most Irvington high schoolers seemed to be wearing lately.

The expression on Rapunzel's face was familiar too. Not at first, maybe; for the first minute she only looked startled and confused. She was talking to the three adults, asking questions, most likely. But then suddenly she was angry again, just like last night. Her talking seemed to have turned into shouting, and the other people in the room were obviously all shouting back. At Rapunzel—and also at each other.

For a while everything was in confusion. Everyone seemed to be yelling at once. Then Rapunzel threw out her arms in a hopeless, almost begging gesture, and covered her face with both hands. Bowing her head so that a thick curtain of hair slid forward to hide her face, she turned her back on the others. With her hands still covering her face she stood perfectly motionless, except that her shoulders seemed to be shaking.

She's crying, Hallie thought. *Why don't they do something? Why are they just standing there?* But then, finally, someone did. At last, the woman went to the girl, put her arms around her, and led her out of the room.

The sun was lower now, and the wavy blue haze in the room was thickening. The two men, alone in the room, were doing nothing at all. Not even talking, or at least not very much. In the same room but definitely not close together, they only went on self-consciously watching each other, occasionally glancing at the door through which Rapunzel and the woman had disappeared.

And Hallie went on watching them. She had been observing the two men and wondering about them for quite a while, maybe several minutes, before she suddenly noticed that there was someone else in the room after all. Someone or, at least, some*thing.*

On the left side of the long room, there seemed to be something behind the smaller of the two couches. Something alive and moving. The first time it appeared, Hallie caught only a fleeting glimpse and then it was gone. She was beginning to think she'd imagined it when suddenly there it was again.

It was at the other end of the couch now, and this time she was sure it wasn't her imagination She had definitely seen . . . something. A creature with a small round head covered with what looked like bristly brown fur was hiding behind the love seat. And whatever it was, the two men seemed not to be aware of it at all. Most of the time it was invisible to Hallie too, except now and then when its head rose slowly and cautiously, first at one end of the small sofa and then at the other.

A dog, perhaps? Hallie wondered. *A round-headed, bristly-haired, brown dog?* But that seemed unlikely. Whatever it was, its movements, its cautious, controlled appearances, seemed undoglike, much too careful and well planned. Its lack of ears was undoglike too. The round brown head lacked anything that looked like ears. Certainly no pointed terrier-type ears, like Zeus's, and no houndlike floppy ones either.

But then, as the head appeared again on the right side of the love seat, Hallie spotted something that did seem to be an ear. Except that it was round and hairless and set too far down on the side of the head— too far down, that is, to belong to a dog.

Hallie was still completely preoccupied with watching for the next appearance of the head, and possibly the body it belonged to, when something brought her back to reality. A slight sound, perhaps the distant thump of a closing door, reminded her of who and where she was and brought her back to the heat and dust and the surrounding walls of the attic's tower room.

A lot of time had passed since she'd arrived in the

attic. Glancing at her watch, Hallie saw that it was four-thirty. Her mother might come home from the savings and loan at any moment. Reluctantly she took her eye away from the spyhole and hurried across the attic.

It wasn't until she was on her way down the stairs that she remembered what she had forgotten to do. She'd forgotten to check to see if the weird feather-trimmed mask was back on the mantelpiece.

8

"So altogether it was quite a day." Paula Meredith finished up her long report on life at the Irvington Savings and Loan, put the latest microwave dinner for two (Mexican food this time) down on the table, and pulled out her chair.

"Yeah," Hallie said. "Pretty bad, huh?" Actually, she hadn't heard that much of her mother's story. There'd been something about a nasty customer and how somebody named Roberta was taken sick and had to be sent home, but Hallie's mind had been pretty much elsewhere.

She finished helping herself to the enchiladas before she glanced up and noticed that her mother was looking at her in a puzzled way. "What is it, Hallie?" she asked. "What's on your mind now?"

"What do you mean *now*?" Hallie twisted her lips in a phony smile. "What kind of *now* are you talking about? Like *now* this minute, or *now* lately, or what?"

Her mother smiled back. "Now this minute, I

guess. There just seems to be something . . . I don't know. Something a bit different."

"Oh yeah? Different?" Hallie tried to sound cool and relaxed. "Different how? Worse than usual, or better?"

"I'm not sure." Her mother was still looking puzzled. "But better, I think. Yes, definitely better. Just as absentminded, perhaps but less . . ." Mom's smile was a little bit teasing now. "Less Eeyorish, maybe."

Eeyorish. It was one of Dad's Winnie-the-Pooh expressions. Dad had a thing about quoting from Winnie-the-Pooh, and an Eeyorish person was one who, like the donkey, was always gloomy and pessimistic.

Hallie frowned. *Eeyorish* was Dad's. And Mom had no right to use it, particularly not about Hallie. To say that "now this minute" she seemed less like a pessimistic donkey.

"So." Hallie forced her words out through clenched teeth. "So you're saying I don't seem as much like a donkey as usual? Is that it?"

Mom sighed and shook her head. "Oh, Hallie." Her voice sounded sad and reproachful, and fed up too. Even more fed up as she sighed again and said, "You know that isn't what I meant. You're just being . . ."

Hallie was thinking, *yes, go on and say it. Say how obnoxious I am and how fed up you are and how much you wish I'd just disappear or—* But right at that moment the phone rang.

Mom jumped up and went off to answer it, leaving

Hallie feeling disappointed at first and then, after a minute, relieved. A little bit relieved that the fight they'd been heading for hadn't happened after all.

The telephone call was a long one, and before it was over Hallie found herself wondering if she really had been acting less gloomy at dinner, and if so, why? What, if anything, was better?

Nothing was, she told herself. Not any better that day or on any day recently. She didn't have any idea what her mother was talking about. If she had seemed less Eeyorish at dinner, it had nothing to do with any sort of change in her life. It simply must have been because she'd had something else on her mind. She had to admit she'd been thinking about the attic and the spyhole apartment and what had been going on there.

She smiled ruefully. Not that what had been happening there in the apartment on the fourth floor of the Warwick Tower Building was all that cheerful and comforting. Not hardly. What she'd seen through the spyhole hadn't been much like watching a TV show about the ideal American family. None of the people she'd seen in that blue-tinged human aquarium had looked particularly happy. Especially not the beautiful Rapunzel.

Hallie couldn't help wondering what had been going on that afternoon. Why had it made Rapunzel cry? And who or what was the little monster, and what had happened to it? Was one of those two angry men Rapunzel's father? What would he do to the other man, the one in the gray business suit? The two of them obviously didn't like each other. Would there eventually be a fight? Or something even worse? And then there was the mysterious creature behind the love seat to think about.

Hallie was so busy wondering that she forgot to consider what she ought to say next about the Eeyore thing. And then, when her mother finally came back from the phone, she made an announcement that put Hallie's mind on a different track altogether. On Saturday, her mother announced, they would be going back to Bloomfield.

"Back to Bloomfield." That was exactly the way her mother put it, but of course that wasn't what she really meant. Not as in "back to live in the town where you were born and where you spent most of your life." Not likely. When she said, "It seems I'm going back to Bloomfield this weekend. Would you like to go too?" Mom was simply talking about a short visit while she took care of some business and saw her old friend Ellen.

Hallie had known right away what Mom meant. Even so, just hearing those words, "back to Bloom-field," made a painful spasm surge through her chest before it froze into a hard, aching knot at the bottom of her throat. The words "back to" must have done it. As if it were ever possible to go *back to* the way things used to be.

9

That evening, in fact that whole night, turned out to be a Ferris wheel of thoughts and feelings—up and down and around and around. One minute Hallie's mind would be spinning about seeing Bloomfield again. Seeing Marty again, and maybe even Zeus and Thisbe. And a little later Bloomfield would be gone without a trace, and the spinning would be about the spyhole apartment and the things she had seen happening there that afternoon. What had been going on among those angry people, and what had happened after she had had to leave?

Less often, but every now and then, Irvington Middle School would have a turn on the Ferris wheel. A quick spin or two about some hard-edged things she might say to her classmates the next time somebody treated her like dirt, followed by a guilty half spin about the homework she ought to be doing. Up and down, round and round: Bloomfield, spyhole, school, and then back to start the rotation all over again.

At some point she got out her books and binder and stared at them while she thought about what it would be like to see Bloomfield again. "Back to Bloomfield"—the words brought an excited rush even though she knew what kind of a "going back" it would be. Going back to look at their old house—now that someone else was living there. Seeing Marty and maybe other old friends—who would probably still be acting as weird as they had at the funeral. Weird and stiff, because nobody knows what to say to miserable people.

And Zeus and Thisbe? What would it be like to see Zeus and Thisbe again now that they belonged to other people? Would Zeus sulk the way he had that time the family put him in a kennel while they were away on the trip to Mexico? And would Thisbe still sit in her lap and do the superloud purr that Dad always called "Thisbe's turbo engine" now that she had gone to live at the Jeffersons' farm way out in the country?

Thinking about her pets reminded Hallie of the doggy-looking whatever that had been hiding behind the love seat in the spyhole apartment. What on earth would have a head that looked like that, and what was it doing behind the couch? The more she thought about it, the more urgent the question seemed, until at last she just had to try to find out something more. Which meant going back to the attic as soon as possible. She actually headed for the kitchen to get the attic key, but when she got there her mother was still working on some papers at the kitchen table. So she had to pretend she'd come for a glass of water.

"Hallie, I thought you were asleep long ago," her mother said, and Hallie had to say she'd been doing homework. Back in her room she did get a little done on her social studies assignment, but when she checked the kitchen again Mom was still there. So she finally had to give up on the spyhole, at least for the time being.

The next day was Irvington Middle School again, and pretty much the same. Not much better or worse. A little worse maybe, as far as her homework grades were concerned, but the other kids were a little less interested in teasing her. Or else it was just that she was too sleepy to care that much whether they were or not.

Saturday came at last, and after an unbelievably long bus ride, she and her mother were once more on the familiar streets of Bloomfield. They passed scenes Hallie knew by heart, stores she'd shopped in and houses and yards she'd visited all her life. Staring out the window, she was immersed, drowning almost, in a flood of crazy, mixed-up emotions. Good ones that came with good memories of happy times and events. And then the others, as she remembered the terrible days that came after that awful morning in June. And then—there was Ellen, waiting for them at the bus stop.

"Darlings!" Big old Ellen wrapped them both in a gigantic hug and herded them into her beat-up Volvo. At first the talk was just about the paintings Ellen had been working on and the ones, both Ellen's and Mom's, that Berry's Antiques had taken on commission. Mr. Berry had hung the paintings in his store and he would get part of the money if anyone bought them. Ellen thought Mr. Berry was going to sell a bunch of Mom's paintings, which would be great if it happened; they certainly could use the money. But Hallie knew better than to count on it.

The thing was, Mom and Ellen had been in art shows together before, and what usually happened was that lots of people bought Ellen's huge blurry landscapes and hardly anyone bought Mom's small, neat still lifes and portraits.

The talk about paintings was still going on when the Volvo turned onto Green Street. Ellen pulled over to the curb and said, "Okay, Hallie. Out you go. The Goldbergs are counting on you for lunch. Emma says Marty's so excited she can't see straight."

So then came knocking on the Goldbergs' front door and lots of kisses from Marty and her parents, not to mention Beowolf, their humongous Russian wolfhound. Lunch was okay because Marty and her parents only talked about things that were happening in Bloomfield, like the new mall and the computer classrooms at Hill Creek Middle School. But then her parents went back to work and Marty took Hallie out to the porch swing for a private talk. Just the way she always used to do, Marty tucked her long legs up under her, rubbed her nose with the back of her hand, and grinned her sideways grin before she began to talk.

At first it felt okay. Hallie was glad to be sitting on the Goldbergs' porch swing again, talking to Marty. At first, but not for very long, because things were not the same and it was no use trying to pretend they were. And it soon became obvious that Marty was pretending much too hard. So the anger had begun to churn around deep down in the pit of Hallie's stomach even before Marty started to run down Hill Creek Middle School.

"Oh, school? It's okay, I guess," Marty said. "An awful lot of homework, though. Lots more than we ever had at Lincoln. And some of the teachers are really old-fashioned and strict." She shrugged and sighed and, watching Hallie out of the corners of her eyes, went on, "I guess you're really lucky to be going to school in Irvington."

That was a lie and they both knew it. Marty had always been a good student and, just the other day, on the phone, her mother had told Hallie's mom how much she liked Hill Creek.

Hallie was getting the picture. The things Marty

61

was saying were just a bunch of lies that were supposed to make Hallie feel better about having to leave Bloomfield. As if Marty thought she was too much of a mental case to deal with the truth.

And it got worse when Marty started talking about Irvington Middle School. Saying things like "I've heard that sixth graders at Irvington can sign up for drama classes, and there's a skiing field trip in February. You're going to go, aren't you? I wish Hill Creek had a ski trip. And drama classes. I'd really like that." That last part, at least, was the truth. Marty had always wanted to be an actress.

Hallie shrugged and said she guessed she would go on the ski trip. She'd made up her mind not to gripe about Irvington to Marty, even if she had to tell some humongous lies about all the new friends she was making and stuff like that. But by then she was so fed up with Marty's treating her like some kind of a basket case, she suddenly decided she was through with pretending. "It's the pits," she said. "I hate it."

That did it. Right away Marty stopped even trying to act normal. Untucking her legs, she sat up straight and began to talk the way she had at the funeral, as if Hallie were some kind of pitiful psycho who might start bouncing off the walls if anybody said the wrong thing to her.

For the next few minutes Marty went on and on, sounding exactly like the counselor Hallie had been taken to see right after the accident. Hallie listened in amazement to the same Marty who used to make up private languages so nobody else could understand what she and Hallie were talking about. And crazy stuff like having a secret hand signal that meant that the next thing you said was going to mean just the opposite. That same Marty went on and on in some kind of school counselor–speak. "I know how that must make you feel. But just you wait. My mom says she had to go to a lot of different schools when she was growing up, and she says all you have to do is hang in there for a little while and . . ."

But by then Hallie had all she could take of Marty the psychologist, so she just tuned her out and started thinking about something else. Like why she'd ever imagined she might be able to tell Marty about her secret spyhole and what she'd been seeing through it. As soon as she possibly could she started pretending that she was expected back at Ellen's right away.

It was a long way from the Goldbergs' house to Ellen's, particularly if you took a detour down Hillview Street as far as number 309. By the time she got to Ellen's, a couple of hours had passed, and Ellen and Mom had been worrying about her.

"Why on earth did you do such a thing?" Ellen roared as she pounced on Hallie like an angry pit bull. "Worrying your poor mother like that. You know I'd have come to pick you up if you'd called me." She was holding on to Hallie's shoulders as if she were about to shake the living daylights out of her, and for a second Hallie really wished she would. Wished Ellen would shake her really hard so she could yell back at her and throw herself on the ground and have a real screaming tantrum. But Ellen didn't do any actual shaking, so all Hallie could say was "Yeah, I know. It turned out to be a dumb idea."

Actually, it had been a whole lot dumber than Ellen knew, or could even imagine. Maybe it had been pretty stupid not to think about Mom and Ellen wondering where she was and worrying about her. But it was even dumber to walk all that way to 309 Hillview Street just to stand there outside the fence staring at the house where she used to live, and at a couple of little kids playing on the jungle gym Dad built for her. And dumbest of all, for some reason, was staring at one of Zeus's beat-up old tennis balls that was still lying under the hedge right where he'd probably left it the day his new owners came to get him.

10

om said Hallie never should have gone to Bloomfield that Saturday, because the way she'd been acting ever since was "absolutely impossible." Hallie supposed she was right. She was right about one part of it, at least: the part about how it had been a mistake for Hallie to go back. But as for "acting impossible," she could see nothing different about the way she'd been acting.

"What do you mean, impossible?" she asked icily. "How could I possibly do something that's impossible?"

Her mother sighed angrily. "*That's* what I mean. Impossibly touchy and quarrelsome and sarcastic." She turned her face away and motioned over her shoulder for Hallie to go away. So Hallie did.

In her room, Hallie sat on her bed and tried not to think about what Mom had said and whether it was really true. After a while she began to think that maybe she had been touchy lately, and maybe she was sorry about it, but there was no way she was going to be able to say so. What she did instead was to go out and ask Mom if there was anything she needed at the store, which in a way was a kind of apology, if only because of the way she said it.

All she actually said was "Hey, Mom. I really need to go to the library. You know, to work on my essay for social studies. I could stop at the store on the way home if there's anything we need." Her smile felt almost real as she went on, "Didn't you say we were out of milk?"

Looking surprised, Mom opened her mouth to say something, but Hallie hurried on. "So would it be okay if I did some shopping?"

Mom definitely looked pleased. Surprised at first, but then mostly pleased. "Why, yes. That would be a big help," she said. "We are out of milk, and the bread is almost gone too."

So that was how it happened that maybe half an hour later Hallie was sitting at a big library table in the East branch of the Irvington Public Library, reading up on the Sinai Peninsula in a junior edition encyclopedia. It wasn't too interesting, just kids' stuff, but when she tried to bring an adult encyclopedia into the children's room the librarian told her she couldn't. Hallie didn't see why not and she said so.

"Oh yeah?" she'd said. "They always let me in Bloomfield. In the Bloomfield library I got to read any encyclopedia I wanted to."

So then the librarian, whose name was Mrs. Myers, said that must have been nice, but rules were rules, and that here in East Irvington the adult encyclopedias were for adults to use. Hallie thought of a sarcastic remark she might have made, but instead she only shrugged and turned away.

It didn't take long to make notes on the material in the junior edition. Hallie was almost finished when a squeaky voice said, "Excuse me. Could I ask you something?"

For just a second she didn't know where the voice was coming from. Not from the old man at the end of the table, which only left whoever it might be almost out of sight behind the big stack of books directly across from where she was sitting.

"Yeah?" she said more or less in the direction of the book pile. "What did you say?"

The top of a head appeared then, brown hair and big dark eyes. "I said, could I ask you something?"

"Yeah?" Hallie said. "Like what?"

More face appeared over the wall of books. A small, toothy mouth and then a pointed chin. "Like, could I see that S encyclopedia when you're through with it?"

She remembered then that she had noticed the kid as she sat down, but just barely. Mostly what she'd noticed was the big pile of books in front of him. A kind of book barricade that had almost hidden him until he sat up straighter and stretched his neck a little.

When she did get a better look at him she was surprised, because he looked so young, for one thing. Probably not more than eight or nine years old. Not nearly old enough for the kinds of books he was reading—or at least hiding behind. Hallie couldn't see any of the titles, but there seemed to be several junior edition encyclopedias plus a lot of the kind of big old dusty volumes you had to ask the reference librarian for. So when the kid's funny face poked up from behind his book barricade and asked for her S volume, Hallie couldn't help grinning.

"Sure," she said, "when I get through with it." She looked his stack of books up and down before she asked, "You in a big hurry? Looks to me like you've got enough there to keep you busy for a while."

The kid glanced at the books before he nodded and said, "Well, I've already read most of these. At least the parts I'm interested in."

"Oh yeah?" Hallie teased with a grin. "Let's see. What parts are you interested in?" She turned her encyclopedia and studied the letter S. "Oh, I get it. Like S for sex? You looking for sexy stuff?"

The kid looked at her for a while before he shook his head. Not angrily like she'd expected, and not embarrassed either. Just a kind of curious stare before he said, "Is that what you're reading about?"

"Who, me?" Hallie put on an offended expression. "For your information, I happen to be reading about the Sinai Peninsula. S-I-N-A-I, with a capital S. Get it?"

"Oh." He nodded thoughtfully. "The Sinai Peninsula. Is the Sinai Peninsula interesting to read about?"

"Yeah, sure. Real interesting. So how about you? If you're not reading about sexy stuff, what are you reading about?"

Looking around at all the books, he nodded and said, "Psychiatry mostly. So far I've mostly been reading about psychiatry."

Hallie let him see she was having a hard time keeping herself from laughing out loud. "Psychiatry doesn't start with an S." She giggled.

"I know." He held up a P encyclopedia. "I've finished with psychiatry for now. Next I want to read about shamanism."

"Shamanism?"

He nodded, pointing at her S encyclopedia. "That's why—"

"*Shhh!*" The man at the other end of the table was staring angrily. "Will you kids shut up!" Hallie made her return stare say maybe she would and maybe she wouldn't.

But when she turned back to her fellow perpetrator, he'd disappeared behind his books again. Only the top of his head was showing behind the barricade, the top of a small round head covered with a furry crop of thick brown hair. Hallie stared in amazed recognition.

But then, before sneaking suspicion could translate itself into for-sure-and-certain, the boy was on his feet and walking away. The smallish eight- or nine-year-old boy was moving quickly, with a lively, bouncy walk, toward the library door.

"Hey, wait!" Hallie called after him, and then, glancing back at the fiercely frowning old man, she cupped her hands around her mouth and whispered it again. "Hey, wait for me!" But he didn't, so after hurriedly gathering up her books, Hallie ran after him.

Outside on the front steps, she stopped to look up and down the street. Up and down, but mostly up, toward Warwick Avenue and the Warwick Towers apartment building. And sure enough, there he was, bouncing along quickly, almost at the corner of Abbot Street. She followed at a run, down Larsen Street, the short block on Abbot, and then onto Warwick Avenue. She was close to catching up, only a few yards behind, when he disappeared into the lobby of the Warwick Towers apartment building.

So she'd been right. The small, fuzzy brown head that had appeared from behind a stack of books in the East branch library was almost certainly the same head that had emerged from behind the love seat in the spyhole apartment. And if that was true, what about the monster in the horrible mask? There was something about the lively, limber way the little monster had bobbed around the room that made her think there might be a connection there too. And if there was—that meant that one of the people who lived in the spyhole apartment was a boy who went around wearing a mask and who hid behind the furniture in order to spy on a bunch of angry adults. And who also read big old books about psychiatry and—what was it he wanted the S encyclopedia for?— oh yes, shamanism.

Shamanism. The word sounded vaguely familiar. On her way back down Larsen Street to the grocery store, Hallie tried to remember what it meant, without much success. So when she passed the library she popped back in again and found out.

Shaman, the dictionary said: *a priest-doctor who uses magic to cure the sick, to divine the hidden, and to control events that affect the welfare of others.*

So that was what it was with the mask—the weird little creature she'd seen struggling with Rapunzel had been a witch doctor? Or maybe Rapunzel's little brother pretending he was one? Yeah, that probably was it. The kid had been pretending to be a shaman, maybe putting some kind of witch-doctor spell on Rapunzel, and she hadn't exactly appreciated it. Picturing what the scene must have been like if she'd caught him doing it, Hallie was surprised to find herself chuckling.

Back in the apartment, Hallie took the milk and bread to the kitchen, and when her mother asked she said yes, she'd gotten the information she needed at the library. "Yeah. I found out some interesting stuff," she said. She couldn't help smiling a little as she added, "*Really* interesting."

The essay on the Sinai Peninsula went pretty well, except that now and then the writing was interrupted by some questions that weren't answered in the textbook or in the encyclopedia. Questions like why would a kid want to dress up like a witch doctor? And what had been going on right before Rapunzel dragged him into the living room? Had she been telling his father on him, and if so, what did his father do to him? And what did he find out when he hid behind the love seat and spied on the three angry adults?

There was a lot she didn't know and wanted very much to learn. But going to the spyhole was out, at least for the time being. Not while her mother was at home. And later, after her mother had finally gone to sleep, the spyhole rooms would undoubtedly be dark and deserted.

So she'd have to wait to find out more. She would wait until Monday, a school day, when there would be that hour and a half before her mom got home. Of course, Monday was also the beginning of another exciting week at good old Irvington Middle School. It didn't seem possible that she was looking forward to it, but in a way she was. Or at least to the other things that might happen on Monday.

11

Monday morning finally came, and Hallie got a B-minus on her essay on the Sinai Peninsula, which was an improvement, even though it would have been one of her lousier grades back in Bloomfield. And what was more, she managed to get through the day without attracting the attention of any of her terrorist-in-training classmates. She might actually have felt like celebrating except that her mind was on something else most of the time—or maybe some*one* else. Someone she started trying to locate as soon as school was out.

Her plan, which she'd been working on all day, was to head for the corner of Warwick and Bruce Street, where anyone coming from the elementary school and heading toward Warwick Avenue was likely to cross. As soon as her last class was dismissed she started for Bruce Street at a run, but she must have been too late, because the fuzzy-headed kid never showed up. Maybe he'd skipped school that day. Or maybe he went to another school, like St. Paul's at the other end of town.

Anyway, since he didn't show up, she finally decided to forget it, at least for the time being. But just in case, she went on waiting at the corner for at least another fifteen minutes before she headed home. Home to the cell block and, even though it was late, to the attic spyhole.

She hurried across the attic. The far corners of the long, empty space were oozing ominous shadows, but with her mother due home in less than an hour there just wasn't time to worry about ghosts. And once she was seated on the old trunk, leaning forward to the blue-glass spyhole, she forgot about ghosts and dry, dusty heat and everything else.

However, the living room of the little witch doctor's apartment was disappointingly empty. And it stayed that way until her time was up and she had to run downstairs to wait for her mother.

The next day at school started out pretty much as usual, but during lunch hour Hallie sat with Erin and another new girl named Jolene. The first time Jolene talked with Hallie alone, she brought up the subject of Hallie's father. They had been on their way to science class when Jolene said she thought it was really the pits about Hallie's father and the big freeway pileup.

Hallie's first reaction had been anger. "Oh yeah? Who told you about it?"

Jolene shrugged. "Erin," she said. "Erin talks about everything."

"So I guess she told you I lied to her about my father?"

Jolene looked puzzled. "Oh yeah? What did you tell her?"

Hallie couldn't believe she was actually talking about such private stuff with an almost perfect stranger. She stared at Jolene for a second, thinking seriously about just turning around and walking off. But in the end she went on walking silently.

"She didn't mention a lie," Jolene finally said. She grinned. "It probably didn't make much of an impression. She's a world-class liar herself."

Hallie nodded. "Yeah, I guess that explains it" was all she said.

Being with the two of them that day in the cafeteria wasn't much of a strain. With Erin and Jolene, most of the time all she had to do was sit there and listen, or at least pretend that was what she was doing. The gossip that day was mostly about this very popular kid named Jason who had been running in a relay race when his baggy cargo pants fell down.

"Yeah, I heard about it," Hallie said. "And he was wearing Batman underpants . . . right?"

"Right," Erin and Jolene said in unison. Then they had another fit of giggling and Hallie laughed a little too, just to be sociable. When her last class was finally over she took off at a run for the Warwick-Bruce intersection.

Quite a few elementary school kids crossed the intersection that day, but not the kid she was looking for. She was on her way home, feeling angry and frustrated, when suddenly there he was, scurrying down the street from the other direction. He was wearing a heavy backpack and clutching a stack of books in both arms. Obviously he'd come home by way of the library, and running after him, Hallie asked herself why on earth she hadn't thought of that possibility. Stopping off at the library was exactly what a nerdy little kid like that would do.

"Hey!" Hallie yelled. "Hey, kid!" He kept right on going, but when she finally caught up and reached out to get his attention, he stumbled and fell. Books went everywhere.

"I'm sorry," Hallie said. And she really was. He'd never talk to her now.

Sitting on the sidewalk, the kid was pulling up his pants leg to inspect his knee.

"Is it skinned?" Hallie asked. He didn't look up for a moment. Too angry, maybe, or else fighting tears. But when he finally did lift his head, it didn't seem to be either. He stared at Hallie for a moment before he asked, "Why did you do that?"

"Do what?"

"Push me down. Why did you want to push me down?"

"I didn't." Now *she* was getting angry. "I didn't *want* to push you. Why would I want to do that? I was just trying to get you to stop."

"Hmm." He looked thoughtful. "Why did you want me to stop?"

The little dork really was frustrating. Totally frustrating. "Look," she said, "I just wanted to talk to you. I wanted to ask you something."

Pulling down his pants leg, he stood up and began to collect his scattered books. "All right. What did you want to ask me?"

"Well, when we were talking in the library the other day . . ." He looked blank. "You do remember, don't you? We were sitting across the table from each other in the library?"

"I remember," he said, nodding solemnly.

"Well, then . . ." What should she say? What should she say that would get him started talking? "Well, then, I was wondering what you've found out about shamanism. I'd like to know about shamanism myself."

"Why is that?"

"Well, just because . . ." She got bogged down for a minute, and when she went on all she could think of to say was "Why do you keep asking *why* about everything?"

"Oh. Why do I ask *why* so much?" He nodded slowly. "Because that's what psychiatrists do, and I might be one someday. Either that or a shaman,

77

maybe. I haven't finished deciding which. I want to be someone who finds out what people are thinking about and why they do the things they do."

"Do shamans do that?"

This time his nod was firm and confident. "Yes. Yes, they do. Just like psychiatrists, only they do it in different ways."

"Like by dancing or doing ceremonies?"

His stare was questioning, suspicious maybe. "Yes, sometimes."

"And do they wear anything special while they're doing the ceremonies? Like special costumes—and masks?"

This time his quick glance was definitely suspicious. "Yes, sometimes."

"Cool," Hallie said. "I like that. I like masks, that is." She tried to make the next question sound like something that had just occurred to her. "Do you have a mask?"

This time his nod was enthusiastic. "Yes. I have one. A really great mask. My uncle gave it to me."

"Oh yeah? Is he a witch doctor?"

His smile was almost a laugh. "No. He's in the navy. He goes to a lot of places. Like to islands in the Pacific Ocean. That's where he got my mask."

"Really? From an island? Tell me about it. What does it look like?"

But suddenly he was gathering up the rest of his books. "I have to go now," he said.

"Wait. Wait a minute," Hallie said frantically. "Don't go yet. Please don't go."

"Umm..." More slow, thoughtful blinking and nodding. "Why not?"

Hallie racked her brain. If she told the truth, if she said "Because I need to find out some stuff about you and your sister," he would ask *why*, of course. And what would she say then? All she could do was stammer, "Because—because I want to talk to you." And then, while his mouth was just beginning to shape itself in another "why," she had an inspiration. "As a psychiatrist, I mean. I've been wanting to talk to a psychiatrist for a long time. So maybe I could be—like someone for you to practice on."

That took a lot of thought, but when the lips finally puckered to form a W sound, what came out was not "why" but "where?"

They wound up sitting on the bench at the bus stop at the end of the block. While that was being decided on, and during the time it took to walk down to the corner, Hallie's mind was racing, coming up with an interesting idea or two. So once they were seated, with the kid's books neatly stacked beside him, she began by saying that maybe, if he was going to be her psychiatrist, they ought to introduce themselves.

"My name is Hallie," she said. "Hallie Meredith. What's yours?"

"Zachary," he said. "I'm Zachary."

But when Hallie asked his other name he shook his head. "Zachary is enough," he said. But then he smiled, a small private smile, and added, "Except for Doctor. Doctor Zachary."

"Okay." Hallie suppressed a grin. "Doctor Zachary. Got it."

"Okay." He took a notebook and pencil out of the side pocket of his backpack. "What did you want to talk about?"

Working on what she ought to say next, narrowing her eyes and chewing on her lip, Hallie put on a deep-in-thought act. "So," she began, "so, Doctor Zachary..." But she had to stop then while she straightened out an even more insistent grin. The crazy little dork was just too funny, sitting there in the midst of all those fat books with a supersolemn expression on his babyish face, and with his great big lug-soled shoes swinging at the end of his short, skinny legs.

"So... how old are you anyway, Doctor Zachary?" It wasn't what she'd meant to say but it just slipped out. If he didn't like the question, it didn't show. At least not so she could notice it. But he did frown a little when she went on, in a teasing way, "And don't ask me *why* I want to know."

"I won't," he said. "I already know why. It's because I don't act my age." He shrugged. "That's what a lot of people say anyway."

"Which is?" Hallie prompted him.

"Nine" he said. "Well, almost nine. My birthday is in November."

So the doctor was going on nine years old. Hallie unbit her lip and then said, "Well, what I've been wanting to talk to a psychiatrist about is..." Suddenly she had a great idea! "Well, it's about these strange dreams I've been having."

The kid—Dr. Zachary, that is—looked almost enthusiastic. The most enthusiastic, actually, that Hallie had seen him look about anything. "Yes," he said approvingly. "Dreams. Dreams are good. What kind of dreams?"

Now she was ready for him. "Well, most of them have been about this girl. This girl who lives high up in a tower, and she has this awesome hair. Long and blond, like, way down past her waist. Only her eyes are very dark. Very big and dark. And she is standing—in this dream, she's standing in this window staring down toward a busy street. And she's looking sad, or maybe kind of angry."

Dr. Zachary was definitely interested. He stared at Hallie for quite a while before he said, "How old is she, the girl in your dream?"

"Oh, I don't know. Pretty young, though. Probably a teenager. Yeah, she's this really gorgeous blond teenager."

"Hmm," the doctor said. "That sounds like my sister."

12

"**Y**our sister!" Hallie tried to sound absolutely amazed. Zachary nodded. "Except for the beautiful part."

"You mean you don't think she is?"

He nodded. "I don't," he said, "but I guess some people do." His forehead wrinkled thoughtfully. "Why would you dream about my sister?"

Hallie shrugged and swallowed a smile. "How should I know? You tell me. You're the psychiatrist."

Zachary's eyes, in fact his whole small, pointy-chinned face, seemed to tighten suspiciously. "I think you know who my sister is. You must have met her somewhere." He looked Hallie over thoughtfully. "Not at her school. You're not old enough. Maybe . . . maybe at the video store?"

Hallie shook her head. "No," she said, "I've never met your sister. Not in person anyway. But I guess I've seen her. You know, in my dreams."

There was another long stretch of silence before he

got up and started gathering his stuff. Hallie stood up too, but after a moment Zachary sat down again. With his backpack on and his arms full of books, he looked at her long and carefully before he said, "Okay. About your dream. Tell me some more about your dream."

"Well, all right," Hallie said. She sat down again very slowly, giving herself time to think. "Well, ... hey, don't you want to put those down?"

He hugged the books to his chest. "No, I have to go in a minute. And besides ..."

"Besides what?"

"I like holding books. My brain works better that way."

Hallie smothered a smile. "Oh well, okay then. So about my dream ..." But her mind wasn't cooperating. After another long pause she said, "Well, in my dream the girl with the hair is a princess, like in a fairy tale, and her name is Rapunzel." Zachary was listening carefully, his eyes wide and staring. When he was listening his face had an eager, hungry look. Or maybe thirsty, as if he were drinking in every word. Hallie smiled at him before she asked, "Do you know that fairy tale?"

He nodded slowly. "I think so. There's a witch in the story, isn't there?"

"Yes, and a prince who is the girl's boyfriend. Only the witch has locked the girl in the tower."

"Why?"

"I don't know why. To keep her from seeing the prince, I guess."

"Oh, yes." He nodded, slowly at first and then faster. "Yes," he said, "that's why. To keep her from seeing the boyfriend. Because he's too old—and has a ring in his nose."

"What did you say?" Hallie couldn't believe she'd heard right. "Ring in his nose? I don't remember anything about a ring in his nose."

He blinked and shook his head like someone just waking up. "Her boyfriend has one. I didn't see it, but my dad did. My dad says anybody who—" Suddenly he was on his feet. "Here he comes," he said. "I have to go." He rushed off toward the Warwick Towers building.

Hallie looked the other way, where a long gray car was approaching. It slowed down as it passed her, and as it turned onto the ramp that led down into the Towers' garage, she got a pretty good look at the side of the driver's head. She thought she recognized him as the man whose feet and ankles always stuck out when he sat in the corner of the spyhole apartment, but she couldn't be sure. She would have been a lot more certain if she could have seen his legs.

Hallie was headed for home when, just beyond the ramp that led down to the garage, she passed the main entrance to the apartment building. She stopped a minute to think, then went back and walked in the door. She'd never been in the Towers building before, not even the bottom-floor shopping mall.

Turning to the left, she passed a shoe store and a women's clothing store called The Warwick Look. Ahead she saw a flight of stairs and some double doors that led into a large room that resembled the lobby of a hotel. There a modern statue that looked like what was left of a pretty badly beaten-up knight in armor, some big potted plants, a receptionist's desk, and, against the far wall, some elevator doors.

A uniformed man on a stool at the high desk looked up as she came in. She was edging back toward the door when he called to her in a businesslike tone, "Can I help you, miss?"

Hallie smiled at him, the wide, crinkly-eyed smile that she knew would make a deep dimple in her right cheek. Her dad used to say she had a smile that could take the starch out of any stuffed shirt. She felt a little bit out of practice, but she gave it a try as she looked up at the man and said, "I don't know, sir. I think this is where my aunt lives, but I'm not sure."

The man smiled back at her before he checked his computer screen. "What's your aunt's name, girlie?" he asked.

She would have to choose an unusual name, she knew. If she said Smith or Brown he probably would call someone up and ask if she was expected. "It's— Sinai," she said. "Mrs. Sinai."

"Hmm. Sinai," he said. "How do you spell that?"

That was easy. "S-I-N-A-I," she said.

"First name?"

"Pen . . . Penelope. Mrs. Penelope Sinai."

He nodded and turned to the computer. While he was scrolling down the screen she looked around for what she'd been hoping to find: a list of the people who lived in the fourth-floor apartments. But other than the list on the computer, there didn't seem to be one. So when the doorman said he couldn't find a Mrs. Sinai, she said she was sorry she'd bothered him. "This must not be the right place. My aunt said it was a big tall apartment house on Warwick Avenue. But I guess I kind of forgot which one."

She smiled again and he gave her a big grin as she turned to go. Back in the shopping mall, hurrying toward home, she was surprised when a couple of little old ladies cooed at her like she was some cute little kid. And she was even more surprised when she realized she must have brought it on by forgetting to get rid of the smile she'd managed to come up with for the doorman. It was the kind of thing that didn't happen to her much anymore.

Wiping the smile off her face, in fact turning it upside down, she stalked out the door and onto the sidewalk. It didn't mean anything, she told herself. She still hated Irvington and everyone who lived there. Nothing had changed, and it wasn't about to.

13

By the time Hallie left the Warwick Towers shopping mall, it was almost four-thirty. Her mother was due home any moment, so a visit to the attic spyhole would have to wait. But on Thursday there would be an after-work meeting at the savings and loan, which meant some extra spyhole time. It would be hard to wait that long, however. Somehow, learning so much about Zachary and the Rapunzel girl only made finding out more seem increasingly important. So important, in fact, that a weird little shiver ran up Hallie's back every time she thought about it.

There were still so many questions to be answered. Was the long-legged man in the chair the same person as the driver of the gray car? And was he Zachary's father, and Rapunzel's too? And who were the other people, the angry man and woman, and what were they all saying when they yelled at each other? What kind of mean, violent things had the three of them been yelling while poor old Zachary was hiding behind the sofa hearing every word of it?

And then there was the other question, the most important one of all: How was she going to arrange another meeting with Zachary? *Doctor* Zachary. She almost grinned. How do you go about getting an appointment with a doctor who is only eight years old? Or as he said, almost nine, even though his birthday wasn't until November.

The next afternoon on her way home from school, Hallie made a detour that took her past the library. But after a quick check showed her that Zachary's favorite table was empty, she hurried home and went directly to the attic. This time she remembered to look right away to see if the witch-doctor mask was back on the mantel—and it was. The strange wedge-shaped head with its enormous white fangs and tall crest of frazzled feathers was sitting right where it had been that first time she looked through the spyhole. And it was definitely the same head she'd seen another time as well, only that time it had been sitting on the shoulders of the little black-robed monster that was fighting with Rapunzel.

She was still checking out the mask when the door directly across from the big window opened and suddenly there he was: Zachary himself. Hallie gasped and almost slid off the trunk, and then wondered why. Why was she so amazed to see Zachary there in the apartment when she was almost sure he was the person she'd seen in the witch-doctor mask and also caught glimpses of behind the love seat? Ever since she'd met him in the library, she'd been certain the little monster, the fuzzy-headed couch spy, and the wannabe psychiatrist were all one and the same person. Even so, it was a real rush to see the familiar big-eyed, knobby-kneed kid bouncing into the blue-lit room. As usual, he was carrying a couple of big books.

Hallie went on staring, feeling as thrilled and excited as if she were catching a glimpse of a movie star, while Zachary crossed the room and stopped for a moment to look up at the mask on the mantelpiece. Hallie held her breath, hoping he'd take it down and put it on. But instead he turned away and, disappointingly, disappeared into the corner of the room that she couldn't see, the corner where the man with the long legs usually sat.

Of course, Zachary's legs were too short to stick out, so he quickly became completely invisible, but Hallie could see him very clearly in her mind's eye, curled up in his father's chair with his nose in one of the fat books. She could picture the chair too. A big, thick-armed leather chair like the one that had been her father's.

She was still picturing the chair and how Zachary looked curled up in it when the door opened again and another person entered the room.

It was the same guy, all right. Hallie recognized the profile she'd seen in the gray car. The same long-legged man who usually sat in the hidden corner was walking across the room, carrying a newspaper in one hand and a glass in the other.

Immediately, before the man had reached the center of the room, Zachary was back in sight too, as if he'd jumped out of the chair and scurried away. It was almost as if . . . Hallie smiled, remembering how Zeus used to act when someone came in and found him sleeping on a chair he wasn't supposed to get up on.

The man turned toward Zachary and began to talk. Hallie could see his lips moving. Then Zachary was saying something back and holding out his book. Maybe telling his father about what he'd been reading. Yeah, that was probably it, holding out the open book and telling his father about it. He was still talking, his lips moving rapidly, when the man turned his back and disappeared into the invisible corner.

Finally Zachary stopped talking. But he was still looking toward the hidden corner where his father was probably sitting in the chair, putting his drink on a side table and shaking out his newspaper. Sure enough, the legs came back in sight then, long legs and big feet in shiny black shoes. Zachary went on standing there, staring into the corner, for a long time before he slowly closed the book, turned around, and went out of the room.

After Zachary disappeared, Hallie went on watching for a while to see if something else was going to happen. But nothing did. Before long she got tired of looking around the bare-walled, boring room and watching the motionless black shoes, and she decided to leave.

She was on her way across the attic when she thought again about the way Zachary had jumped up, and how it had reminded her of Zeus. She started to smile again, remembering Zeus's guilty-faced retreats, but the smile fizzled out suddenly when she decided it wasn't really all that funny. It was funny when a dog got up and scurried away looking guilty, but a kid who did it when his father came into the room . . .

It wasn't until she was going down the stairs that she started smiling again, this time remembering how, when she was a little kid, she used to fight with her dad over his big leather chair. She would try to beat him to the chair when he got home from work and when she won he would pretend to sit on her, and she would scream and kick and they would both yell and laugh. Usually the game ended with her sitting on his lap while they read a book or the comics or sometimes just discussed really important things. Things like having conversations with God, for instance.

Some people, even good friends like Marty, would kid her when she told them about the things she used to say to God, but Dad never did. Dad said everybody talked to God in one way or another, and he thought the kind of chatty, neighbor-to-neighbor way she did it was just fine.

But that brought back other memories, the ones about how many times she'd asked God why He had let Dad be a part of the accident on the foggy freeway. God hadn't ever answered that question no matter how many times she'd asked it, and after a while she'd stopped asking Him anything at all. When she got back to the hot, stuffy apartment she was crying angry tears again, but this time they didn't last very long.

By the time her mother got home, Hallie had stopped crying and had started thinking about how she could find out how often and on what days Zachary stopped at the library on his way home from school. When her mom asked how her day had been she said the usual "Oh, okay, I guess." But then, for some reason, she had a sudden urge to talk to Mom about Zachary. Without spilling the beans about the attic and the spyhole, of course.

"Mom," she started out, "something funny happened on the way home the other day. This little kid, who I'd kind of met at the library—he came along carrying a whole bunch of books and all of a sudden he fell down and the books went everywhere and . . ."

Mom winced. She'd always been that way about kids or animals getting hurt. "Oh dear," she said. "I hope he wasn't—"

"No. He wasn't hurt. Not really. Just a skinned knee. But I started talking to him and we wound up sitting on the bus bench talking about a lot of stuff. And Mom, this little kid, he's only eight years old, is really pretty weird. He reads all these big books about things like psychiatry and shamanism. . . ."

"Shamanism?"

"Yeah, do you know about shamans?"

Mom nodded uncertainly. "Not a great deal. Only that they are something like wise men, or gurus."

"Yeah, like that, sort of. I didn't know either, so I looked it up. But this kid says that the reason he's interested in being a shaman is that they cure mental cases who need to get their heads straightened out. Like being a psychiatrist, sort of. That's the other thing he thinks he is—a psychiatrist. I think he wants to be a psychiatrist because they get to ask people a lot of personal questions. You know, like how they feel about things and why they feel that way." She smiled, remembering. "*Why* seems to be his favorite word."

Mom laughed and Hallie laughed too. "He sounds like quite a character," Mom said. "Does he live near here? In the Towers, maybe?"

Hallie quickly looked up at her mother. Dad used to say that he was married to a mind reader, and sometimes Hallie thought he wasn't just kidding. She tried to make her shrug say she didn't know and didn't really care where he lived. "Could be," she said. "I guess an awful lot of people live there."

Watch it, Hallie. Better change the subject. Better cool it about Zachary, and anything else that might bring up the spyhole.

14

The next day Hallie visited the library again, but not to get a book. At least, that wasn't the main reason. The main reason was to see if she could get some information about Zachary's library habits. She did check out three more books on the Middle East, but they were mostly for cover, and to get Mrs. Myers in a friendly state of mind. Which was something that probably needed doing, since Hallie had insisted on telling her how much better everything was at the Bloomfield library. But now, since she was definitely going to need Mrs. Myers's help, she picked out some books figuring that librarians were probably friendly to people who checked out lots of research-type books.

Sure enough, the librarian in charge was Mrs. Myers again, but she didn't seem to recognize Hallie when she handed over the three books. "Hello, Mrs. Myers," Hallie said, flashing her best starch-removing smile. "I was wondering if a little boy named Zachary has been in the library today." The librarian was shaking her head. "He has short brown hair and he's about this high." Hallie held out her hand to show Zachary's height. "He comes in here a lot to read books about stuff like shamanism."

The librarian had begun to nod. "Oh yes, that Zachary," she said, smiling. She ran Hallie's books across the scanner. "So you're looking for Zachary Crestman." She turned Hallie's card over and glanced at her name. Then, looking puzzled, she asked, "You're not his sister?"

"No." Hallie discarded the smile as she said, "I'm *not* his sister." She couldn't hold back an impatient sigh as she added, "Does that matter?"

"Oh," the librarian said, "I remember you now." Her eyes narrowed. "The Sinai Peninsula, wasn't it?" She glanced at Hallie's card again. "Why do you want to—?"

"I just want to see him, okay?" Hallie was feeling frustrated. "I just wanted to . . ." She paused, trying frantically to think of a good reason why she should be given information about Zachary, but nothing came to mind. She briefly considered saying "His sister asked me to give him a message." But then, what if the librarian wanted to know his sister's name? She was still hesitating when, just at that crucial moment, the phone rang. Making a "wait just a minute" gesture, the librarian turned her back and began to talk on the phone. Hallie picked up her books and walked away.

She was fuming as she ran down the front steps of the library. Angry at the nosy librarian, for one thing, but mostly at herself for blowing it. For not managing to find out anything except . . . except . . . what was it she'd called him? Zachary Crestman. So that was his last name. She *had* managed to discover something after all. By the time she got home, she had another plan in mind. A plan that involved the telephone.

There were, it turned out, three Crestmans in the Irvington phone book. One of the listings gave an address that wasn't on Warwick Avenue, so that left just two. No one answered at the first number she dialed, and the answering machine message gave the names of the people who weren't home right then. There was no Zachary, so that left just one possibility. Triumphantly, without stopping to figure out what she was going to say—impulsively, Ellen would say—Hallie punched in the number.

"Hello, who is it?" The voice sounded young and breathless. Was it Zachary? No, more like a girl's voice. A teenager's voice, maybe? Realizing that she was probably talking to the mysterious Rapunzel made it even harder to think clearly.

"Uhh . . ." Hallie hesitated, frantically trying to decide what to say.

"Hello," the voice said again, and then even more softly, almost in a whisper, "Tony? Tony, is that you?" Before Hallie had time to say anything at all, there was a quick gasp, and the voice that was probably Rapunzel's whispered, "Oh, I have to go. I have to hang up." There was a *click* and then the dial tone.

So that was that. Another plan down the drain. For a moment Hallie felt mostly frustration, but only for a moment, until it began to change into a curious thrill. What was it Zachary had said when they were pretending to talk about the princess in the tower? That the witch, or her father maybe, wouldn't let her see the prince because he was too old and had a ring in his nose. Hallie shivered. Maybe the prince's name was Tony, and Rapunzel had thought the phone call was from him, her forbidden prince. But then she had to hang up quickly because she heard her father approaching. Hallie put down the phone feeling strangely excited. In a weird sort of way, it was as if she'd become a part of some crazy modern fairy tale.

Back in her room, Hallie got out an old writing tablet. She tore out the scribbled-on pages and started to make a list of what she had found out so far. The List of Facts wasn't very long.

Family's last name: Crestman.
Address: fourth floor of the Warwick
    Towers—don't know the number.
Boy: Zachary.
Age: eight years.

She thought a minute and then, grinning, she erased the last two words and wrote *almost nine, in November*. And then there was . . .

> **Girl: [blank space].**
> (Obviously, her name wasn't really Rapunzel.)
> **Age: teenager, maybe about fifteen?**

So that was about all she knew, except . . .

> **Girl's boyfriend: Tony???**
> **Nose ring.**
> **Pretty old for a fifteen-year-old girl.**

Anything else? No, that was all. Except that there was definitely something weirdly wrong with the Crestman family. Something that made three adults stand around yelling at each other with their hands clenched and anger screwing up their faces. Something that made an eight-year-old kid scurry around like a guilty dog, and made a girl hang up the phone without even finding out for sure who was calling.

Hallie stared at the list, thinking about all the other stuff she really needed to know. Then she jumped up, slid the tablet into her school binder, and ran to the kitchen. A moment later, with the key in her pocket, she was heading for the attic stairs.

15

Hallie wasn't expecting much. There hadn't been much going on lately in the spyhole apartment. Not during the hours when she could watch, anyway. But the urge to check it out, to be sure she wasn't missing something important, was suddenly too strong to resist. If she didn't visit the spyhole today, she might miss a clue that would let her know what was really happening to Zachary and his family.

But once again it turned out to be wasted effort. Nothing moved in the bleak, watery blue room. Entertaining herself by lifting and lowering her head to make the light swirl in blue waves, Hallie stuck it out until almost four-thirty before she gave up and headed back across the attic.

She had locked the door to the attic stairway behind her and was opening the door to her own apartment when a familiar voice called her name.

"Hallie, dear, how good to see you."

Hallie whirled around to see a white-haired lady

dressed in a baggy sweatsuit and a wraparound polka-dot apron making her way up the stairs from the second floor. It was Mrs. Tilson, of course.

Hallie flinched, her mind racing. If Mrs. Tilson had seen her coming out of the attic, she was really in trouble. She was, at least, if the old lady decided to tell on her, to blab to Mrs. Crowley or, almost as bad, to tell Hallie's mother what she had seen. And why wouldn't she want to tell? Why wouldn't she want to get someone in trouble who had been so—whatever it was Hallie had been that day when she delivered the Tilsons' yogurt, ate their cherry pie, and then blew up and stormed out. Wondering what the old lady could possibly be doing up on the third floor, Hallie shoved the attic key in her pants pocket and reluctantly turned back.

"Oh, hi," she said. "I—I just got back from school."

"Yes, yes. So I see, my dear," Mrs. Tilson gasped. She was carrying a large cardboard box, and as she neared the top of the stairs she seemed to be badly out of breath. When she finally reached the third floor she took another deep breath and panted, "Oh my! Too many stairs." She went on puffing for several seconds before she added, "But what a lovely coincidence. I called just a few minutes ago to ask if you could give me a hand, but there was no answer. And then here you are, as if by magic."

"Give you a hand?"

"Yes. A helping hand to get this box up into the

attic." She held out the heavily taped box. "That last flight up into the attic is awfully steep."

"Oh," Hallie said. "Oh yeah. I can carry it up for you. I carried a lot of boxes up there for my mom when we first moved in." As she took the box she grinned and said, "But I guess you know that, according to Mrs. Crowley, I'm not supposed to go up there by myself." Remembering some of the comments the Tilsons had made about Mrs. Crowley, she thought she knew what the reaction would be, and she was right.

Mrs. Tilson shook her head, making indignant *tsk-tsk* noises. "That Crowley woman," she said. "So many rules. Harold says ..." She smiled, giggled almost. "Harold calls her Mrs. Moses, because every time she shows up we get ten more commandments."

Still giggling, Mrs. Tilson unlocked the attic door and handed Hallie the box. "Just put it with the other cartons labeled Tilson. And then do come down for some cookies and lemonade."

Up in the attic Hallie found the right stack of boxes and then headed back down the stairs, trying to think of a good reason why she couldn't go on down to the Tilsons' apartment. She didn't want to go, but it wasn't really because of what had happened the last time she was there. At least not entirely. It was more that she had other things on her mind, like the list she'd been working on.

"So." Mrs. Tilson's rabbity pink nose twitched

daintily. "How about our little visit? Harold is volunteering at the museum this week and I'm so tired of being all by myself."

"I don't know," Hallie said too quickly. "I'd like to, but my mom will be home real soon, and she'll worry if I'm not here."

"Well now, I think I might..." Mrs. Tilson was fishing around in her apron pocket. As she pulled out a pencil and a scrap of paper she went on, "I think I might have a solution to that problem right here."

An embarrassingly obvious solution, and one that Hallie should have thought of, of course. It was pretty much too late now to come up with a more reasonable cop-out, like too much homework, or an important phone call she was expecting. Giving up, Hallie scribbled a note for her mother, left it on the kitchen table, and went on down to the second floor.

Once they were inside the apartment, Mrs. Tilson insisted that Hallie make herself comfortable in the living room while she went into the kitchen to get their "little treat."

It really was comfortable in the Tilsons' apartment. A lot cooler than on the third floor, and an awful lot cooler than in the attic. Hallie had been in the Tilsons' living room several times before, but never all by herself. Left alone, she wandered around the big, bright, high-ceilinged room, checking out the ornate molding around the fireplace, the neat antiques, and the fancy gold-framed paintings. And then there was the tower room.

While the tower rooms on the third floor and in the attic were nothing more than barren alcoves, this one was an important part of the Tilsons' living room. The drapes on the curving windows were beautiful, heavy and shiny, and below them a circular window seat was built right into the tower wall. Above the window seat were wide panels of stained glass. Kicking off her shoes, Hallie knelt on the window seat and stared out through green glass leaves and yellow petals.

On her left a leaf-shaped pane looked across the air well directly into the Warwick Mall's dress shop. Remembering the store from her visit to the mall, Hallie examined it again, noticing how much more interesting it was when everything and everybody, even the air itself, was tinted a deep jungle green. Seen through the green glass, the racks of scarves and dresses had a kind of rain forest feel, and if she squinted, it was easy to see the clerks and customers as rather well-dressed iguanas.

Turning slightly, Hallie discovered that by peering through a patch of yellow, she could look straight down on Warwick Avenue. It was rush hour. The yellow glass gave the air a sunny sheen; the street was full of cars with lemon-tinged windows, and on the sidewalk, all the passersby had glowing golden skin.

Golden men walked by in business suits or blue jeans, and then came a group of beautifully gilded young women in short skirts, long jackets, and brightly colored scarves.

There were gangs of kids too. Teenagers mostly; girls in short dresses and clunky, thick-soled shoes, followed by a straggle of tall, lanky boys with bristly hair and wide, baggy pants.

And then, right there among all those ordinary-looking teenagers, there was a girl whose hair was a shimmering, sliding curtain of brilliant gold. It looked like—it had to be—Rapunzel. Rapunzel and—could one of the boys be Tony? The Tony whose name Rapunzel had whispered before she quickly hung up the phone, and whom she had been forbidden to see because of unimportant things like his age and the ring in his nose? There seemed to be three—no, four boys in the group, and from the second-floor window it was hard to check out all their noses.

Pressing her own nose against the glass, Hallie moved back and forth, trying breathlessly for a better view as she watched Rapunzel and her friends stroll on down the street and disappear into the Warwick Towers mall.

Hallie's nose was still flattened against the yellow glass pane when the sound of footsteps and the clink of glasses brought her back to the reality of Mrs. Tilson's approach with cookies and lemonade. Quickly putting down the tray, she joined Hallie at the window and peered out through the colored glass.

"What is it?" she asked as eagerly as an excited first grader. "What did you see?"

"Nothing," Hallie said quickly. And then more slowly, "Nothing special, that is. Just someone I thought I knew."

Kicking off her shoes and tucking up her feet like a kid, Mrs. Tilson twisted around and looked down Warwick Avenue just as Hallie had been doing. She went on staring for a minute or two before she turned around and said, "I always like looking out windows. Don't you?"

Hallie thought for a second before she answered. "Yeah, I guess so." And then without planning to, impulsively maybe, she asked, "How about looking *in* windows? How do you feel about looking into other people's windows?" The words were hardly out of her mouth before she was second-guessing herself, wondering why she would ask such a dangerous question.

Mrs. Tilson glanced at Hallie quickly before she smiled and raised her shoulders in a guilty shrug. "Why, yes. I guess I really do." She lifted her shoulders again in a kind of shudder. "I've always liked looking in windows and wondering about the people who live there and guessing what might be happening in their lives. It gives one the shivers, doesn't it?"

Actually, Hallie agreed about the shivers. She'd felt that thrill creep up her backbone before, particularly lately when she was wondering about Zachary and Rapunzel, but it didn't seem wise to admit it. Instead she pretended to be shocked. "You mean you like to peek in other people's windows?"

Mrs. Tilson was busy now, pouring the lemonade out of a tall silver pitcher into two glasses, but she stopped long enough to look thoughtfully at Hallie. "Why, I guess that all depends. Yes, I think it does. What one likes depends on so many things. But what I do think . . ." She paused again, nodded, and then went on, "I do think looking out—looking out at other people is a very healthy thing to do." With her small white head tipped to one side and her eyes glazed and unfocused, she went on, "Yes, much better than looking at yourself all the time. Like in mirrors, for instance."

Hallie didn't get it. "You mean, like, windows are healthy because of the fresh air?"

Mrs. Tilson was smiling as she handed Hallie a tall, ice-misted glass. "Yes, that's a part of it. A kind of freshness might be a part . . ."

The doorbell was ringing. "Oh my, there's the bell. That must be your dear mother. I'll just go let her in."

Hallie jumped up saying, "I'll go. Let me go."

As she hurried to the door, she was feeling relieved, glad to get away. The conversation had started to get a little bit weird.

16

Two important things happened in the next few days. The first was that somebody finally showed up again in the spyhole apartment. Hallie had been there for at least a few minutes on every school-day afternoon, but no one was ever there. It was almost as if Zachary and his family had suddenly moved away, leaving the bleak, bare-looking apartment looking even more lonely and desolate. But on Thursday, when Hallie's attic time was nearly over, there she was again. Rapunzel.

It was another very hot day. Rapunzel was wearing a scoop-necked T-shirt and a short denim skirt, and her heavy hair was tied back off her neck. She burst into the room suddenly and immediately darted right to the window. Then, just like before, she stared down toward the avenue. But this time something had changed about her face. It took Hallie a moment to realize that it was mostly her eyes that looked different, red and wet-lashed and surrounded by dark smudges that might be bruises—dark, smeary bruises around both of her tear-wet eyes.

Standing there at the window, so close Hallie almost felt as if she could reach out and touch her, the poor tragic Rapunzel stared at the avenue below, pressing her cheek to the glass. Her lips were moving, saying something—the same word, over and over again. Then she turned around and ran out of the room.

Hallie stayed at the spyhole awhile longer, trying to move her own lips in the same way. Trying to find out if Rapunzel could have been whispering "Tony, Tony, Tony."

That was it, all right. That was exactly what she'd been saying. Sitting there on the trunk, sweating in the dusty, airless heat, Hallie thought about the poor imprisoned princess and her forbidden love. She practiced saying "Tony, Tony, Tony" over and over again in a despairing voice. She stayed there quite a while, pretending to be a poor tragic princess, wishing her hair were long and blond instead of short and brown. She might have stayed even longer if it hadn't been for the heat.

The second more or less important development happened the very next day, when Hallie left school a little bit later than usual because she happened to run into Erin and Jolene on her way out of the building.

They both squealed when they saw her, and Erin yelled, "Hallie, where have you been? We've been looking for you."

"Oh yeah?" Hallie slowed down. "What's up?"

Erin giggled some more before she said something that sounded like "We need to ask you something."

It was hard to know for sure because at the same moment Jolene was giggling and saying, "You know, for our gossip column."

Hallie was in a hurry but she stopped to listen. The gossip column in the weekly school newspaper had been Jolene's idea, but Hallie had agreed to help with the writing, because, as Erin put it, "you're the best writer in our whole class."

But when Hallie asked what they wanted her to write, they said they only wanted to ask her a question for a poll they were taking.

"Okay. So what do you want to ask me?" Hallie said.

It turned out that the question they were researching at the moment was—giggle, giggle, giggle—who else in their class was in love with Jason Johnson, besides both of them.

Hallie said she didn't think she could be much help on that one, except that she herself wasn't, so they could cross her off their list. It was easy to see that Erin and Jolene were disappointed. Hallie thought of adding that personally, she thought Jason Johnson was a conceited jerk, but she decided against it. She finally managed to get away by saying she had to go because she had an important errand to run on her way home.

The errand Hallie had in mind was one she'd been doing every day lately, which was checking the library to see if Zachary was there. So far there had been no sign of him. And today after spending so much time with Erin and Jolene, she almost didn't bother to stop. But in the end she did, and there he was at his old spot, surrounded by his usual stack of books. Hallie felt a breath-catching relief to see the funny little nerd sitting there looking the same as always—followed by an urge to tease him a little to get even with him for making her worry. She picked up a book to pretend to be reading before she pulled out the chair across from him, sat down, and whispered, "Hi. How's the witch-doctoring business?"

He looked up quickly and then, without smiling at all, he said, "Oh, it's you. I've been wanting to see you."

Hallie grinned. "Well, that's a coincidence. I've been wanting to see you too."

Still not smiling, he tipped his head to one side and solemnly asked, "Why?"

Hallie laughed out loud. "Hey," she said. "You said you wanted to see me first, so I get to ask why first. Why did *you* want to see *me*?"

He nodded. "All right. I wanted to see you to ask you some more questions about dreams. Sometimes dreams are very important."

For a split second Hallie didn't know what he was talking about. Then she remembered how she'd told him about dreaming a kind of Rapunzel story about his big sister. "Oh yeah," she said, "about my dreams." She paused and then went on cautiously, "You mean my dream about Rapunzel?"

He nodded and then shook his head. "About my sister," he said. "About Tiffany. I wanted to know how you could be dreaming about someone you didn't even know, so I've been looking on the Internet to find out about psychiatrists who study dreams. I found out about psychiatrists like . . ." He picked up a couple of the books and showed them to her. One of them was *Memories, Dreams, Reflections* by Carl Jung, and the other was *The Interpretation of Dreams* by Sigmund Freud.

"Wow," Hallie said. "Can you understand that stuff?"

Zachary stared at one of the books and then at the other. "No," he said, frowning thoughtfully. "Not yet. But I'm going to."

Hallie was opening her mouth to say "Yeah, I'll bet," when she suddenly gulped and shut it again. *Wow,* she was thinking, *he said "Tiffany." So her real name is Tiffany.* For just a split second she felt disappointed. The name wasn't right. Rapunzel shouldn't have a faddish modern name like Tiffany. It ought to be something with a fairy-tale sound to it, like Aurora or Elsbeth.

111

But at the same time, she felt good about making such an important discovery. Triumphant even. So triumphant she forgot to watch what she was saying. "Tiffany," she murmured. "Tiffany Crestman." The moment she said "Crestman," she remembered that it had been the librarian who let Zachary's last name slip. Zachary had never told her, had refused to tell even when she came right out and asked him. And sure enough, he was giving her a narrow-eyed stare.

"You said *'Crestman,'* " he said. "How did you know our last name?"

Hallie cast about frantically for a good answer and came up with a pretty unbelievable one. "I—I don't know," she stammered. "I guess it was a part of my dream."

Zachary's eyes got even narrower. "You dreamed our last name?"

Swallowing a smile, Hallie nodded firmly. "Yes," she said. "I guess I must have. How else would I have found out what it was? I mean, you wouldn't tell me."

Zachary got out a notebook and pencil, opened the notebook to a new page, and smoothed it down carefully. "Okay. Tell me about the dream," he said. "The one that had 'Crestman' in it."

"Well, all right. The Crestman dream." Hallie rolled her eyes, trying to look as if she were deep in thought, when what she was really doing was looking for some way to change the subject—or for somebody who might change it for her. Like the grumpy old man who had made them stop talking, or maybe Mrs. Myers. There was no sign of the old man, but the librarian was a definite possibility.

Raising her voice to an unlibrarylike pitch, she went on, "I had that dream just last night. I was dreaming about this tower where the princess lives and down at the bottom of the tower was a knight in armor."

"A knight?" Zachary asked. "On horseback? Was the knight on a horse?"

Hallie shook her head. "No, I don't think so. I don't remember a horse. But I was in the dream and I went up to the knight and asked him if I could see the princess, and the knight had this magical scroll with a lot of names written—"

Someone tapped Hallie on the shoulder. She looked up to see Mrs. Myers bending over her and whispering, "Could you two keep it down a little?"

"Oh, okay. We're sorry," Hallie said. But inside she was saying *Whew! Just in time.* And it really was. She hated to leave before it was her turn to ask questions, but she knew she'd better cool it for the time being. Her Crestman dream was definitely getting out of control, and she had a feeling Zachary knew it.

She was standing and picking up her book when Zachary reached out and took hold of it. "Wait," he mouthed. Then he tore off a part of the page he'd been writing on and handed it to her. On the page in fat, primary-grade cursive he had written I DON'T THINK SO.

Hallie gave him an indignant frown, but he didn't frown back. Instead he just went on looking at her with his strange superfocused stare. After a minute her frown started changing into a grin. Turning the page over, she wrote OKAY, YOU WIN. I DON'T THINK SO EITHER.

Zachary smiled, grinned actually. He nodded and she nodded back. Then she grabbed the paper again and wrote OKAY. HOW DO *YOU* THINK I FOUND OUT?

At first Zachary only shrugged and shook his head. Then his smile disappeared and his funny, pointed face suddenly scrunched into a pitiful hangdog look that reminded Hallie of Zeus when he was feeling really unhappy. After he'd stared accusingly at Hallie for a long moment, he bowed his head until Hallie couldn't see his face and began to write. Began to write slowly and stiffly as if he could hardly make the pencil move across the paper. It took a long time and it was, as Hallie noticed impatiently, even more impossible to read his wobbly cursive letters upside down than it was to read them right side up. When he finally finished writing, he sat staring at the paper for a long time before he slowly turned it around. What it said was I THINK YOU READ IT IN THE NEWSPAPER.

Hallie glanced at what he had written and wrote READ WHAT?

Zachary took it back. OUR NAME he wrote. IN THE
NEWSPAPER.

Hallie grabbed the paper and wrote WHY? WHY DO
YOU THINK

But before she finished writing she realized that
Zachary was gone.

17

Hallie left the library feeling disappointed and frustrated. She'd finally found Zachary again and talked to him, but she'd come away without learning very much. It wasn't until she was almost home that she began to ask herself why it mattered so much. Why exactly had she spent so much time looking for Zachary, and why did she need to know the answers to the questions she had been planning to ask him? After all, the weird little kid had nothing to do with her. It was, she decided, nothing more than simple curiosity. She was just curious about Zachary, and the rest of his family, too.

About Rapunzel—oops, *Tiffany*—in particular. Tiffany and her boyfriend, that is. She had to admit she was more than a little curious about them. Who wouldn't be? Who wouldn't want to know why a gorgeous teenage girl would stand at the window looking down at the street with bruised red eyes whispering "Tony, Tony, Tony"? And why would she hang up the phone so quickly when she obviously thought it was Tony calling?

But Rapunzel/Tiffany wasn't the whole story. There were a lot of other questions that Hallie wanted answers to. Questions about Zachary and his long-legged, angry-faced father. And now there was a new and even more mysterious question: Why would Zachary think she'd learned his last name by reading something about it in the newspaper?

What exactly had been in the newspaper, she wondered? What had the Crestman family done that reporters would have been interested in writing about? Thinking back to the angry scene she had watched from her spyhole, it occurred to Hallie that right at that particular moment something pretty awful might have been about to happen.

That night, after she'd finished her homework, she had some new stuff to add to her List of Facts. For instance:

> Girl's name: Tiffany.
> Other clues: The Crestmans have been
>   written about in the newspaper.
> Things to do: Find out what the newspaper
>   article said. (How? How do I find out?
>   Library, maybe??)

At first, the library did look like her best bet. It seemed to Hallie that she'd read about detectives

117

looking stuff up in old newspapers. But as far as she could remember, the stories didn't tell how they went about doing it. Especially if they didn't know the exact date of the edition they were looking for. You might ask the librarian, of course, but probably not if you were a kid. And especially not if your local librarian already thought you were a real pest.

Hallie went to sleep that night without solving the newspaper problem. But the following Monday morning she stumbled on what might turn out to be the answer. An answer source that was always full of information. Her name was Erin.

It was lunch hour, and Hallie was eating at the same table with Erin and Jolene as usual. Erin had been carrying on about the results of the poll to find out how many girls in their class were in love with Jason Johnson.

She jumped up once and hurried across the room, and when she came back she opened a little notebook and wrote in it, a name with a number after it. "See that?" She was pointing to the number. "I just got Allison Anderson. That makes thirty-eight."

"Thirty-eight." Hallie laughed. "How can there be thirty-eight? There are only thirty people in the whole class, and half of them are boys."

"Oh, it's not just a class poll anymore. We're doing, like, the whole school," Jolene said.

"Yeah." Erin's blue eyes glittered with enthusiasm. "And then we're going to do McPherson Middle

School too. And then maybe all the other schools in town."

"Okay, okay," Hallie said. "If anyone can do that, it would have to be you. After all, your mother knows everybody in—"

"Yeah, like, in the whole city." Jolene got up from the table and took some coins out of her pocket. "Excuse me, everybody, I'm going to get some apple juice. Don't go away. I'll be back in a minute."

But Hallie had stopped thinking about the Jason poll. What she was thinking now was that if anybody knew why the Crestman family had been mentioned in the local newspaper, it would have to be Erin Barlow.

"Everybody in Irvington." Erin finished Hallie's sentence for her. "Well, it's true. My mother knows everybody in Irvington, and now that she's on the city council and everything, she gets to meet important people all the time. Like last week, when—"

"Okay, okay," Hallie interrupted her. "So what do you know about some people named Crestman?"

"Crestman?" Erin frowned. "I don't remember hearing about—"

"They were in the paper," Hallie said. "There was something about them in *The Irvington News*. Something bad, maybe. Like . . ."

Erin's eyes had gone glittery again. "Like murder, maybe?" she asked.

"No. I don't think it's *that* bad," Hallie said. "Just

something you wouldn't want people to read about. If it were your family, I mean."

Erin wrinkled her forehead and narrowed her eyes. She nodded slowly a few times before she said, "Oh yeah, I think I remember. I think that was the name of the man who robbed the National Bank. And he shot someone too. Like maybe a guard or something. Yeah, that was his name. Crestman."

Hallie couldn't help gasping. Her mind was racing. She felt shocked, horrified, and then, watching Erin's jittery eyes, suddenly suspicious. "Are you sure?" she asked.

Erin nodded confidently. "Yeah, I'm sure. Crestman. That was his name. It was in *The Irvington News*."

Right about then Jolene came back with her apple juice. "Crestman?" she asked. "Are the Crestmans in the newspaper again? What is it this time?"

"You know the Crestmans?" Hallie asked.

"I don't know them, but a man named Richard Crestman used to work where my dad did. But then this Crestman guy's wife got a divorce and there was like a big fight over who was going to get to keep the kids and the house. Stuff like that."

"That must be it," Hallie said. "Was it in the paper?"

Jolene nodded. "Yeah. My dad was reading about it in the paper when he told us about this guy he kind of knew from work."

"When was that?" Hallie asked.

"Oh, I don't know. Not long ago." Jolene was looking at Hallie curiously. "Why do you want to know about the Crestmans? Do you know them?"

Hallie shook her head. "No, not really. I just heard someone talking about them. He said they lived somewhere around here. Do they? Do you know where they live?"

Jolene shook her head. "Don't ask me. Somewhere in Irvington, I guess."

Erin was poking Jolene impatiently. "Come on, Jolene," she kept saying. "Let's go poll Mr. Hardison's class."

As they started off Erin looked back over her shoulder. "I still say there was a murder. My mother knows all about it."

18

That afternoon Hallie waited a long time at the library, but Zachary never showed up. By the time she got home it was already after four o'clock. There was so little spyhole time left she almost decided not to bother. Standing in the middle of the kitchen, holding the attic key in her hand, the reasonable side of her personality pointed out that there wasn't much chance of anything happening in the Crestmans' apartment in the next fifteen minutes. But the other side, the impulsive one, kept reminding her that she hadn't seen the apartment or any of the people who lived there since she'd found out that they'd been written up in *The Irvington News.* And that there had been a divorce, at least, and maybe even a murder, in the family. In the end, the impulsive side won.

As she hurriedly climbed the stairs and crossed the attic, everything seemed the same as always. The same empty shadows and dry, dusty air. But somehow she had a sneaky feeling that something was wrong. Wrong, or at least different. She was almost to the tower alcove when she did notice one small change: About halfway across the long, dark space, she saw what was obviously a new stack of trunks and boxes and even a few pieces of furniture.

She didn't know why, but for some reason it really bothered her. She stopped for a moment to wonder and worry before she suddenly remembered something that explained the difference. Just that morning at the breakfast table, Mom had said that a new family was moving in to one of the second-floor apartments. So that explained it. The new stuff must belong to them. Nothing to worry about. That was what she told herself, anyway. Only there was a part of her that didn't seem to be listening and kept right on worrying. And that turned out to be the part that was right.

There definitely *was* something to worry about. Hallie had no sooner reached the tower room and sat down on the old trunk than she was startled by a strange clicking sound, followed by a lot of other noises. Sitting on the trunk, frozen with surprise and fear, she began to realize what she was hearing. The grating click had been the attic key and the other sounds were voices and footsteps on the stairs. One of the voices belonged to Mrs. Crowley, Mrs. Moses Crowley with all her rules and commandments and her power to decide who got to live in the Warwick Mansion and who didn't.

Afterward Hallie couldn't remember how she got unfrozen enough to move at all, or how she managed to wind up in a heap between the trunk and the tower wall. But she apparently got there somehow. She did remember the rest of it fairly well.

Crouched down on the splintery floor behind the trunk, she heard the footsteps and voices becoming louder and clearer as they made their way across the attic. Most of the time it was Mrs. Crowley's loud, raspy voice quoting some of the same rules she'd mentioned to Hallie and her mother. Rules about the kinds of things you were allowed to store in the attic and the things you weren't, as well as the kind of people who weren't allowed to visit the attic, like anyone who wasn't a renter. And children. Particularly unaccompanied children.

Hallie crouched lower, her mind whirling helplessly. Spinning briefly into burning anger, a fierce, fiery resentment at being labeled a child. Anyone, even someone as dense as Mrs. Crowley, ought to be able to understand that no one could be a child again once they'd lost everything that had been good about their childhood.

But anger was only part of it. Only a small part. Mostly there was fear of what might happen to her if old Crowley found her hiding there in the attic's tower room. What might happen to her, and to her mother too. What if they were kicked out of the Warwick Mansion, so that Mom would have to start looking all over town again for the kind of crummy apartment they could afford to rent? Looking at awful places, worse even than the Warwick Mansion servants' cell block. More run-down and worn-out and ugly and . . . The thought hit her hard: And it would have no blue-glass spyhole, and no hope of ever finding out what was happening or might happen to Zachary and Tiffany Crestman.

Crouching down even lower, she tried to condense herself into an even smaller space, to melt into the attic's dusty shadows until she disappeared. Until there was nothing left to be discovered and denounced and thrown out of the attic for good and always.

Crowley and her new renters were taking forever. There were scraping noises, as if the newcomers were moving their things around, and over it all the high-pitched rasp of Crowley's voice giving directions and quoting and requoting all the rules and commandments. At last the noises began to fade and the sound of footsteps retreated across the attic and finally down the stairs.

Hallie stayed in a tight little ball behind the old trunk until the faint clicking sound of the key turning in the lock drifted through the shadows and the attic was once again its old, silent self. As she slowly unwound herself and got to her feet, she surprised herself by whispering something she hadn't said for a long time. "Thank you. Thank you." She didn't say out loud who she was talking to, but He was right there on the tip of her tongue. Running on tiptoe, she headed for the stairs.

Safely back in her own kitchen with the attic key returned to its shelf, she was surprised and relieved to find that her mother still wasn't home. And then surprised again to discover that it was only a minute or two after four-thirty. Which would seem to mean that the eternity she had spent hiding behind the trunk had actually only lasted somewhere around ten minutes. She was still standing there staring at the kitchen clock when her mother walked in carrying her purse and her heavy briefcase.

All Hallie said to her was "Hey, Mom. You're home." But there might have been something unusual about the way she said it, because Mom looked a little bit surprised. After she put all her stuff down on the kitchen table, she put her arm around Hallie's shoulders and gave her a quick hug. "Right," she said. And then in a tone that made it sound a little like a question, "And so are you?"

It was several days before Hallie could get up the nerve to visit the spyhole again. Days for the new renters to get settled in and stop taking up stuff to store in the attic, not to mention the time it took for Hallie to get over having to hide from Mrs. Crowley behind that trunk. Hiding was something she never wanted to do again, that was for sure. Not any kind of hiding, not any place. Not ever.

In the meantime, however, she did spend a lot of

time thinking about all the things she needed to learn about the Crestmans. Things such as what had been in the newspaper article and whether it concerned a divorce, or maybe something a lot worse. But now that the spyhole wasn't a possibility, there was only one place to go to find out: the library. To the library to look for Zachary.

19

Beginning the very next day after her close call in the attic, Hallie began to be the East Irvington library's most faithful visitor. Every single day after school she took the short detour that brought her to the library's big blank facade, climbed the steps, and went in. And once there, even though Zachary obviously wasn't, she usually hung around until almost four-thirty, hoping he might show up. She tried to find library-type projects to do so as not to arouse the suspicion of anyone who might be wondering what she was up to. Like Mrs. Myers, for instance.

The first project that she really got into was looking up some of the books that had been her favorites back in Bloomfield, where she had always won all the awards for reading the most books. A few of them, on rereading, seemed childish and boring, but some others were just as good as she remembered, or even better. As if there were things an older person could get out of the story that a little kid might miss. And when she got tired of reading fiction, she decided to read up on some of the ancient civilizations they'd been learning about in social studies.

She also began to get better acquainted with Mrs. Myers. Hallie knew Mrs. Myers had considered her a world-class pest, and for a while the feeling had been mutual. But things began to change when Hallie started getting interested in ancient civilizations, and it turned out that Mrs. Myers was too. Either Mrs. Myers just liked people who were into ancient civilizations, or else Hallie's unstarching technique worked on librarians as well as it did on stuffed shirts.

But still no Zachary. Hallie was really getting tired of worrying about what might have happened to him and his sister when, on a Friday afternoon, there he was again, trudging into the reading room wearing the same state-of-the-art backpack and the super-clunky lug-soled shoes. Hallie surprised herself by wanting to rush over and grab him and ... and she wasn't sure what. Hug him, or maybe just give him a good hard shake.

She didn't do either one, of course. Instead she just went on hiding behind some bookshelves. He had settled down at his usual table and was taking some books and papers out of his backpack when she walked over and pulled out a chair.

"Well, look who's here," she said. "Where on earth have you been? I've been wanting to talk to you."

Zachary looked up, stared for a minute, and then,

very solemnly, said, "I have to talk to you too." He looked over at the checkout desk before he went on, "Maybe not here, though."

Hallie agreed. There was no use getting Mrs. Myers all worked up again. Not after she'd just started to calm down. "Okay," she said. "Let's go."

"Where?"

"Oh, I don't know. Maybe out in front of . . ." She had been going to suggest sitting on the library's front steps, but on second thought she began to change her mind. Sitting out on the front steps with a dorky-looking eight-year-old, where everyone who walked by . . .

Zachary got up and started collecting his books and papers. "Come on," he said. "We can pretend we don't know each other."

She grinned, thinking, *Smart kid—smart* psychiatrist *kid.*

So they wound up sitting at one end of the wide marble steps, close enough for each of them to hear what the other one was saying but far enough apart to make it look as if they weren't together. Zachary reached over and handed her a book. "Here," he said. "If you see anyone you know, pretend to be reading. I will too."

Yeah, smart kid.

"Okay," Zachary said while Hallie was still getting settled, "okay. What I want to know is, how *did* you find out what our last name is?"

Hallie grinned at him. "Well," she said, "I told you once, and you didn't believe me."

"I know." Zachary nodded. "I still don't. People can find out lots of things by dreaming, I guess. But mostly things about themselves. Not stuff about other people, like their last names. I didn't read anything about how you could find out other people's last names by dreaming about them."

"Okay, you got me." Hallie grinned. "I didn't dream it up. Actually I found out—" She paused and then, watching Zachary closely, she went on, "I really did find out there was something about your family in the paper, though. Just like you said."

Zachary nodded, but not the least bit triumphantly. "I thought so," he said. Then he looked away, hiding his face. Hallie could only stare at the back of his fuzzy head as she strained her ears to hear what he was saying. "Yes, it was in the paper," he whispered. "But it wasn't true. Not all of it, anyway."

Forgetting about pretending they weren't sitting together, Hallie scooted closer. "What wasn't true?"

"The part about..." His voice was even fainter now. "The part about them hitting each other. She wasn't the one my dad hit."

Hallie leaned closer. "Who...," she began, and then stopped. She couldn't see his face, but judging by the sounds he was making and by the way his shoulders were moving, she was pretty sure he was crying. She was just deciding not to ask any more questions, at least not right away, when he began to talk. His voice was shaky and full of tears as he said, "My dad didn't hit my mother. The paper lied about that. The only one he hit was her lawyer."

Hallie scooted again and put her hand on his shoulder, but he pulled away. "Don't," he said. "Somebody might see you." Then he jumped up and ran down the stairs.

Late that night Hallie got out her List of Facts and, sitting cross-legged on her bed, she got ready to jot down all the things she had just learned. At the top of the second page she carefully printed a heading.

NEW FACTS:
  I. There really was an article in *The Irvington News* about the Crestman family.
    A. About a murder?
       1. Erin says there was one but I don't really believe it.
    B. One thing the article must have said was that Zachary's father and mother had a bad fight, and that he hit her.
       1. Maybe not the truth. According to Zachary his dad only hit her lawyer.

Hallie read over what she had written, but when she got to that point she stopped. According to Zachary... Suddenly she stopped reading and sat perfectly still for a long time, thinking about what Zachary had said and how miserable he'd sounded when he'd said it. Then she ripped out the page. She didn't know why exactly, except that she was remembering something that had happened just a week after her father died.

Right after the freeway accident, Ellen had insisted on taking Hallie to talk to the school counselor, even though school was out for summer vacation. While they were talking, the counselor wrote a lot of stuff in a big notebook that she tilted up so Hallie couldn't see what she'd written.

Hallie had hated Ellen that day for thinking she was helping when she should have known there was nothing anybody could do and there never would be. But she'd hated the counselor even more, with all her careful questions and sneaky note-taking.

So she wasn't going to write down any more notes about Zachary and his family. But that didn't mean she was going to stop trying to find out what might be going on in the Crestmans' apartment, and why Zachary had been crying about it.

20

Unfortunately the next day was Saturday, which meant there wasn't much chance to find out anything for two whole days. Zachary had never been at the library on a weekend, and the spyhole wasn't much of a possibility either. The spyhole problem on weekends was, of course, that Mom was usually at home. But that wasn't the only obstacle. Now and then, when Mom let Hallie stay home while she was out on an errand, Hallie had sneaked upstairs for a quick look, and there had never been anything going on in the spyhole apartment. Nothing at all. It was almost as if the Crestmans lived somewhere else on weekends.

Hallie had almost given up on the spyhole until Monday but then, unexpectedly, Sunday became a possibility because of Ellen. Ellen, it seemed, was going to be in Irvington on Sunday, and she wanted to take her dear friends, Paula and Hallie Meredith, out for brunch. Or Paula, at least, if Hallie had other things to do.

Hallie didn't want to go. She knew that all her mother and Ellen would do was talk about art and people back in Bloomfield, neither of which she wanted to hear about. Mom wanted Hallie to go, but she managed to get out of it by bringing out all the library books on ancient civilizations that Mrs. Myers had found for her. Piling the books up on the kitchen table, she pointed them out to Ellen and Mom and, without exactly saying so, she managed to give the impression that she'd checked out the books because of a humongous homework assignment that she really needed to get started on.

It was about ten-thirty, just a few minutes after Mom and Ellen went out the door, when Hallie started up the attic stairs. It was the first time she'd been there since she'd hidden behind the trunk and, just as she'd feared, some of that awful trapped and helpless feeling came flooding back. At the top of the stairs, she stopped to calm down and to check things out.

Nothing much had changed except for the heat. Now that summer was over the attic was a little bit less like an enormous oven, but the air was still heavy with ancient dust. Tiny dust motes floated in the bands of light that filtered through the dirty windows, and in the far corners, way back under the slanting ceiling, the shadows deepened into pools of darkness. And the ghosts? She smiled. It had been a long time since she'd really worried about Mrs. Crowley's bashful ghosts, but now that they'd come to mind, Hallie kept her eyes on the darkest shadows as she made her way toward the tower alcove.

No sign of ghosts and, just as she'd feared, no signs of life in the Crestmans' apartment. As usual on weekends, the bleak, bare-walled rooms seemed deserted. Hallie had been sitting on the trunk for several minutes, looking through the spyhole now and then, and in the meantime going over everything she'd learned about the Crestman family, when suddenly something happened. Something entirely unexpected.

She had just leaned forward and put her eye to the spyhole again when, from only a few feet away, a face stared back at her. Shocked and frightened, she quickly pushed herself away from the spyhole and covered it with both hands.

The face hadn't been a familiar one. Not Zachary's or his sister's, certainly. She was sure now that what she had seen was the face of a man. The face of a complete stranger who had seemed to be staring back at her from just outside the tower window. But of course that was impossible. Slowly and cautiously she took her hands away from the spyhole and leaned forward.

The face was still there, but now, seeing it more

calmly, Hallie realized that the man it belonged to was not floating in midair outside the tower room, as it had seemed to her at first. Instead he was inside the Crestmans' apartment, standing at the window just as Tiffany had done when she had looked down toward Warwick Avenue. And like Tiffany, the man was not staring back at Hallie. He was only standing in the window where the sun fell on his face, looking out at nothing in particular with a blank, unfocused stare. As she watched, he turned his eyes up toward the sky, then straight across the narrow air well toward Hallie's spyhole, and then down again toward the ground four stories below. Gradually the blank stare tightened into a frown that narrowed his eyes and slanted his heavy eyebrows. Angry eyebrows, Hallie thought, and then she caught her breath in surprise.

The man wasn't a stranger after all. She had seen him before several times, talking with Zachary, and arguing with other angry people, and once driving a gray car. But she had never before seen him face to face, and certainly not when he was so close to her. She was sure now that the wide-jawed face, with its dark eyes and heavy eyebrows, belonged to Zachary's father.

Yes, it was Zachary's father, dressed in a bathrobe, holding a cup in one hand and staring angrily at the outside world. Then, as Hallie watched, holding her breath, he turned away, put the cup down on the table, and went to the built-in cupboard on the far wall. His back was to Hallie now and he was farther away, but she could see his arm move as he pulled open a drawer and reached into it. Turning quickly, he crossed over into the living room area and disappeared into his hidden corner.

Before long his feet and lower legs came back into view as they always did when he sat down, but she hardly noticed them. Her mind was too full of other things. Full of one question in particular: What had Zachary's father taken out of the drawer? What was the small, dull black object that had been partly hidden by his big hand as he crossed the room and disappeared into the corner? Hallie hadn't seen it well enough to be sure, but for some reason she felt certain she knew what it was.

"He's got a gun," she found herself whispering. "He's sitting there in his chair with a gun in his hand." She nodded and then whispered it again before she jumped up and ran across the attic, down the stairs, and back to her own apartment.

Back at home in her cell block apartment, Hallie put the key on the shelf and then stood in the middle of the kitchen without moving even a finger while her mind raced in crazy circles that began and ended with the same two questions: What was about to happen to Zachary and his family? And what should she, what *could* she, do about it?

She didn't know the answers, didn't know any

answers except... Her eyes turned to the old-fashioned dial telephone. She would call. Call the same number she'd used when Tiffany had thought it was Tony calling. And then... She didn't know, and there was no time to think about what might happen next, no time to do anything except dash into her bedroom, pull out the Crestman notebook, and look up the phone number. And then rush back to the kitchen.

What was she going to say? She didn't know and there was no time to decide. The phone had begun to ring before she'd even tried to think about it. What would she say to Tiffany if she answered, or to Zachary? Or to...

"Hello." Someone was answering. Someone with a deep voice. A man's voice. "Hello." And then once more with a questioning rise, "Hello?"

"Hello," Hallie gasped. "Is Zachary there? Could I please talk to Zachary?"

"Who is it, please?" the deep voice said.

"It's, it's..." Not Hallie. Some other name. "It's—" She sputtered again and then came up with "Susie. I'm Susie. I'm in Zachary's class. At school."

"I see." A long pause. What was he doing or thinking? Why didn't he answer? "I see," he said again at last. "Well, I'm afraid Zachary isn't here right now. Could I take a message?"

"No. No, I don't think so. It's just that..." She was calming down a little, her brain getting back to work, even reminding her to make her voice higher, more like an eight-year-old instead of an almost-adult sixth grader. "It's just that we're working on the same project at school and there's something I have to ask him." She stopped to think and then went on, "Could I call back later? When will he be back?"

"Not until Monday, I'm afraid. Zachary is never here on weekends. He should have told you."

"Oh. Okay. I guess I forgot. I guess I can ask him Monday. Thank you. Good-bye." Hallie put the receiver back on the phone and collapsed into a kitchen chair.

So Zachary was never there on weekends. Or maybe that wasn't true. Maybe his father was lying and there was some other reason why Zachary couldn't come to the phone. Shutting her eyes, Hallie went over the conversation in her mind, trying to remember exactly what the man had said and, at the same time, imagining how he might have looked when he said each thing. She could picture him clearly now, the wide mouth and the dark eyes almost hidden under the frowning eyebrows.

And the gun? Was the gun still in his hand when he came to the phone, or had he left it there by his chair? There was no way of knowing.

Hallie sat at the kitchen table for a long time before she remembered Mom and Ellen and what she had told them about the books on ancient civilizations. Picking out the one on the Ch'in Dynasty in

China and the terracotta warriors, she took it to her favorite reading spot in Dad's leather chair.

It wasn't really homework. Actually, they were still finishing up on Rome in Mr. Montoya's social studies class, and she'd already finished her projects except for drawing a map of the Roman Empire. But last week in the library Mrs. Myers had turned her on to this book about the weird emperor who'd ordered the construction of an enormous life-sized clay army. It was a pretty interesting book but, at that moment, not quite interesting enough to keep her attention from wandering. From drifting back to what she had just seen through the spyhole window. Her mind was still flickering back and forth between a cruel emperor and Zachary's armed and dangerous father when Ellen and Mom came home from their brunch.

21

When Mom and Ellen came in they were jabbering away, talking mostly about the art that had been on the walls in The Gallery, which was the name of the restaurant where they'd just eaten brunch.

"I can't imagine why they're showing that Rupert woman's stuff," Ellen was saying to Hallie. "Nowhere near as good as your mother's work." And then, turning back to Mom, she went on, "Like I was saying, you should take some of your stuff over there right away and—"

Mom was shaking her head. "No," she said. "Now stop it, Ellen, you know I can't. You know I don't have nearly enough finished work for a show." But Ellen kept insisting and finally Mom said, "Well, all right, I'll think about it at least, if you really think I should." She paused, her eyes going dreamy and unfocused as she stared into space. "I have been wishing I could find the time to do some painting again." Her lips twisted into a smile that was probably meant to look happy but wound up looking more like an apology. "Maybe just a small still life or two." She looked around the tiny room before she went on, "There must be someplace here that I could set up my easel. Don't you think so, Hallie?"

At first Hallie was surprised, and then a little bit pissed off. Mom hadn't said a word about painting since they'd stored all her painting stuff in the attic when they'd moved into the Warwick Mansion. If she'd been dying to get back to it all this time, she should have said so.

Hallie shrugged. "A place where you could set up your whole studio?" She looked around. "Well, not in here. That's for sure. But maybe in the living room if we move things around a little. Wait a minute." She jumped up and went to look, and when she came back she told them she'd found a place that might work. "If you could paint in the afternoon when you'd get a little better light."

So Mom and Ellen had to check the place out and decide just where the easel and the palette stand could go. Hallie went back to Dad's chair. She was only pretending to read at first but after a while she really got into how the hundreds of warriors in the terracotta army were copies of real people, and one story was that the emperor had all the sculptors killed afterward so they wouldn't give the secret away.

After Ellen left, Mom went in to change her clothes, and when she came out she was dressed in an old paint-smeared work shirt of Dad's that she used to wear as a painter's smock. Hallie hadn't seen the shirt since Dad died and she must have been staring at it, because Mom looked down at it too.

"I know," she said, running her hands down over the paint-spotted denim. When she looked up there were tears in her eyes. Hallie put her book down and stood up.

"So," she said, "I guess we're going up to get your painting stuff."

Mom sniffed and blinked before she said, "I thought maybe I'd bring a few things down. You don't need to help if you don't want to."

Hallie shrugged. "Come on," she said. "Let's get it over with."

It was strange being in the attic with Mom. Hallie had to remember to look around curiously and say the kinds of things she might have said if she really hadn't been there since that first day with Mrs. Crowley. Things like "Wow. Pretty dusty, isn't it." And "I guess those ghosts old Crowley was talking about are on their day off."

On the way back downstairs Mom carried the easel, Hallie the big box of painting stuff. Then Mom went off to the tower room that was probably going to be called the studio now instead of the living room. Hallie went back to reading. At least then she wasn't thinking about Zachary's dad and the gun.

What she really didn't want to think about was

what Mom was doing. She didn't know why, except it had some connection with how Ellen was always talking about things getting back to normal.

Back to normal. Hallie got up, threw her book down on the chair, went into her room, and collapsed on the bed. "Normal," she whispered angrily. "Normal. Yeah, sure." How could things ever get back to normal for Hallie Meredith? Or for Dad? "Yeah, how is that going to work?" she asked out loud, talking to Ellen, who wasn't there. Or maybe to God, who probably wasn't either. "Tell me that. How are things going to get back to normal for Alexander Meredith? Who used to be my father, in case You've forgotten."

But the anger didn't last the way it used to, even though she tried to hold on to it. And this time, when it was gone, she didn't start crying. But that didn't mean anything. Certainly not that things were getting back to normal. All it meant was that, at the moment, there were too many other things on her mind. Things like Zachary's father and what he was planning to do with that gun.

Monday finally came and sure enough, Zachary was right there in the library when Hallie went looking for him. And this time it was pretty clear that he was looking for her too. He almost jumped out of his chair when he saw her come in, and as soon as she sat down he leaned forward and whispered loudly, "Did you phone me? Yesterday. Did you talk to my dad yesterday?"

"Me?" Hallie said. "How would I do that? You didn't tell me your phone number."

Zachary's dark, pointy eyebrows tipped downward. "I don't know how you did it but it must have been you."

Hallie grinned. "You mean you don't have any school friends who might have called you up?"

"Aha!" Zachary said. "See, that proves it. It was you!"

"Why does that prove anything?"

Zachary looked triumphant. "Because my dad told me that the person who called said she was a friend from school. How did you know about that, if it wasn't you?"

Hallie winced and glanced over her shoulder at the checkout desk. Zachary's triumphant voice had been getting louder and louder. And sure enough Mrs. Myers was looking toward them. In another minute she'd be heading their way. Hallie got up and picked up her books, but before she turned away she bent over Zachary to whisper, "Meet me outside on the steps. Okay?"

Zachary nodded and whispered back, "Okay. I was just about to say it. Out on the steps."

A few minutes later they were sitting on the front steps of the library, close enough to talk but far enough apart to pretend they weren't together if anyone who knew them came along. The first thing Zachary said was "Okay. Was it? Was it you who called me up?"

Hallie shrugged. "Yeah, it was. I called you up."

"Why?" Zachary's eyebrows were scrunching down over his big, dark eyes. There was something catlike about Zachary when he frowned. Something that made her think of the way Thisbe used to go all fierce-faced when she was pretending to chase something, even when she was still just a kitten. Hallie had always liked Thisbe's wildcat act, and Zachary's was kind of cute too.

Hallie grinned at him but he didn't smile back. She sighed. "Well, to tell you the truth I called you up because I was worried about you."

Zachary's frown faded into his superfocused stare. "Why?" he said.

Hallie said it in unison with him. "Why? Yeah, I know—why? Well, let's see. I guess you're asking why I was worried about you," she said. "Is that it? Why was I worried about you?"

She wished she could lay it all out. That she could say "Well, the thing is, I saw your father getting something that looked like a gun out of a drawer in your apartment, and I was just wondering what he was going to do with it." But of course she couldn't. She was still trying to think of a good way to explain what had worried her when Zachary said, "Was it something you dreamed?"

Hallie almost said "Hey, I thought you didn't believe my dream story." But then she realized that talking about her "dreams" might be a good way to find out what she wanted to know. So what she said was "Well, actually it sort of was. It was—well, it was one of those mixed-up dreams that don't make a lot of sense, but there was something in it about a—gun. Does someone in your family have a gun?"

She was watching Zachary's face closely as she asked the question but it didn't tell her anything at all. He just went on staring at her wide-eyed and unblinking. "See, in this dream I saw someone in your house, in a living room it looked like, with a gun in his hand."

He still showed no reaction except for a slow, uncertain shake of his head. So Hallie went on, "I was afraid that this person I dreamed up might have shot somebody and that was why I called. But then when your dad answered I just asked to speak to you, only he said you weren't home. He said you weren't ever home on weekends."

Zachary shook his head. "No. That's not right. None of that is right. There's no gun, and I *am* home on weekends. I'm always home on weekends. It's my dad who isn't." Hallie was just opening her mouth to ask him why on earth his father would lie to her, when he said, "Now it's my turn."

"Your turn?"

Zachary took a stubby pencil and a little notebook

out of his backpack before he nodded, looking very solemn. "To ask the questions."

"Questions? What kind of questions?" Hallie asked suspiciously.

"Questions about you." He looked Hallie over critically. "You ought to be relaxed, like on a couch or something."

Hallie snorted. "On a couch? Why should I be on a couch?"

"Because people need to be relaxed when they answer questions." He tipped his head to one side and, with a thoughtful expression on his face, he looked Hallie up and down. "You don't look very relaxed," he said.

"Well." Hallie was getting angry. "I guess that's because I don't feel very relaxed. I mean, get real, kid. How am I going to relax sitting out here on some stone steps, where somebody I know might walk by any minute and see me. . . ." She trailed off before she said "talking to a weird little dork." But just barely before.

For the next minute or two they just sat there glaring at each other. At least Hallie was glaring. What Zachary was doing was more like his usual laser-beam psychiatrist's stare, only this time the facts he was getting ready to record were going to be all about Hallie Meredith herself, not her dreams. Finally she managed to say through clenched teeth, "Okay, now that I'm relaxed, what do you want to ask me?"

Zachary glanced at his notebook. "Well, the first thing I wanted to ask you was who else you have dreams about, besides me and my family. Do you ever dream about your own family? Like maybe your own mother or father? Do you ever dream about your own father?"

That did it. Jumping to her feet, Hallie said, "Forget it, kid," and took off down Larsen Street at a run.

22

Hallie was almost back to the Warwick Mansion before she cooled off enough to start thinking. Thinking and wondering about what had been going on and why she had reacted the way she did. One thing was for certain: That silly little nerd definitely thought he was a psychiatrist.

She shrugged angrily. Well, let him. Let him think that a little third-grade kid knew enough about people to help them solve their problems. She knew better. And one thing she knew for sure was that she wasn't going to tell a dumb little kid anything about herself and her mother and father just because he was a wannabe psychiatrist. And she wasn't going to worry about him anymore either. About him or his gorgeous sister or their weird father. And she certainly wasn't going to waste so much time on the stupid blue-glass spyhole anymore.

And she didn't either. Not on that afternoon or on Tuesday. By Wednesday she was beginning to change her mind, just a little. During the day at school she found herself wondering what might be happening to Zachary, and Tiffany too. She just about decided to make a short visit to the spyhole as soon as she got home. But as she was leaving school she ran into some people she knew who were on their way to the downtown mall and they asked her to come too.

There were four of them, Erin and Jolene and two other girls from her first-period language arts class. Those other two were part of the gang that Hallie had really hated when she first came to Irvington. The kids who used all the secret in-group slang and wore expensive clothes that were the latest thing. A tight bunch of dudes who especially liked to show off for each other by dissing people who didn't belong to their group. Dissing people like Hallie Meredith, for instance. At least that was what she'd thought about them for a while.

After she'd gotten to know some of them a little better, she decided they weren't all so bad, particularly a girl named Katlyn McKnight. Katlyn was along that afternoon, and she and Hallie laughed a lot at Erin and Jolene, who were walking all the way to the mall because they'd heard that Jason Johnson sometimes went there on Wednesdays. So while Hallie and Katlyn shopped for some colored map-making pens, the rest of them shopped for Jason Johnson. The whole trip was kind of interesting even though nobody found what they were looking for, and Hallie barely got home before her mom did. So no spyhole time that day either.

But then on Thursday Mom had an after-work meeting again, which for Hallie meant an extralong afternoon with nothing much to do. Sitting alone in the dingy apartment, she was feeling bored and gloomy, almost the way she felt in the days when she used to wind up looking for a place to hide. It had been a long time since she'd done the hiding thing. Still, she might have started doing it again except that her hiding urge kept getting interrupted by worries about Zachary. Particularly about his father and the gun. That was all she needed. A whole new problem to worry about. She didn't remember deciding to go to the attic, but suddenly there she was, on her way up the stairs.

Just as she thought it would be, the spyhole apartment, at least the part that she could see, was deserted. Nothing moved in the ugly, bare-walled room. She was prepared for that. In fact, she'd brought along a flashlight and a book to read while she waited to see if anyone was going to show up.

She sat on the old trunk for several minutes, reading a page or two, or trying to in the dim light, before leaning forward to take another look. Then, just as she was about to give up and go downstairs, things began to happen.

The man appeared first. For some reason, just watching the tall, dark-eyed man walk calmly into the room made Hallie catch her breath. Her heart began to beat faster. She didn't know why. He didn't seem to be angry this time. No fierce scowl or clenched fist, and the only thing he had in his hand, in both hands really, was a bunch of paper. Maybe a folded newspaper or a bunch of mail.

As always, the man was headed directly for the out-of-sight corner of the room. And just as before, right after he disappeared, his feet and ankles came back into view. Nothing more happened, but Hallie went on feeling tense and nervous, as if she somehow knew there would be more. She tried to read a little between spyhole checkups, but it was harder to concentrate now. After a while, she gave up on the book and concentrated on watching, even though there was nothing much to see. Nothing moved in the watery blue light except for the long legs uncrossing and then recrossing themselves now and then. Hallie was feeling more and more certain something was about to happen, when suddenly it did. The door opened again and Zachary came in.

Just inside the door he stopped to look around. When he turned toward the window Hallie could see him very clearly, with his pointed chin and his wide-set eyes under the fuzzy cap of hair. Compared to his tall, broad-shouldered father, Zachary looked particularly small. Small, quick, and as twitchy as a nervous animal. Hallie found herself wanting to reach out and tap him on the shoulder and whisper something that might calm him down. Something like "Hey, it's okay. I'm right here."

Zachary looked around the room. As Hallie watched unblinking, he moved past the hidden corner and then back again and then slowly, uncertainly, walked toward it and disappeared. For what seemed a very long time neither he nor his father came back into view.

Hallie pressed her forehead against the crack in the wooden paneling and stared until her eyes began to blur and she had to shake her head and blink rapidly to clear her vision. She was just leaning back to the spyhole when Zachary exploded out of the corner and bounced across the room. Whirling around, jumping and dodging, he bounced into the dining area and straight to the sideboard. Jerking open the drawer, that same long drawer she had seen his father open, he pulled something out. Holding it in both hands, he waved it around wildly as he ran back to the hidden corner.

What was it? What was he holding? Hallie couldn't be sure. His hands covered most of it, but the part she had seen was dull black and had a squared-off, blunt shape like . . . Hallie didn't move. She couldn't seem to take her eye away from the spyhole, even though once again, there was nothing to see. But while her eyes saw nothing except the empty room, her mind was seeing a whole series of imagined scenes.

Violent scenes, most of them, in which Zachary was holding the black gun above his head, and then pointing it at . . . Could she hear a gunshot from inside the double-paned windows of the apartment building? She wasn't sure. Another scene appeared in which Zachary's dad was slumped in the chair while Zachary stood in front of him and a curl of smoke drifted up from the black blur in his hands. And one more, in which the father grabbed Zachary's arm and wrestled the gun out of his hands. Pulled it away and then . . .

A strangely unmeasurable amount of time passed. The frightening images flashing through Hallie's mind were so vivid that when somebody finally appeared she was, for a moment, uncertain whether he was real or imagined.

Imagined? No, definitely real. It was Zachary's father. Blank-faced and empty-handed, he strode across the room and disappeared through the door that led to the hall. Several minutes passed. Nothing else moved, no one else came into view. More images began to appear behind her eyes. Images of Zachary, alone now in the invisible corner. Alone, lying limply in the chair, eyes closed and . . . But then his father came back.

Standing in the doorway, he turned toward the invisible corner. He was saying something, his lips were smiling and then moving quickly, pausing and moving again, and then he was gone. And Zachary was running after him, still clutching the strange black object in both hands.

Still holding her forgotten book and flashlight, Hallie sat on the old trunk for only a few seconds before she jumped up and ran across the attic and down the stairs. Not even stopping at the door to her own apartment, she ran on down the second flight and the first and then out on to Warwick Avenue. She was still running when she got to the main entrance of the Warwick Towers building.

23

The elevator guard in the lobby of the Towers apartments looked startled as Hallie burst through the door and skidded to a stop in front of his desk. A skinny, bony-faced man with a ponytail this time. Not the one she'd met before when she'd made up the story about having an aunt who lived in the building. That was good. That, at least, was good.

"Yes, can I help you?" the man said as Hallie gasped and panted, swallowed hard and then blurted out, "The Crestmans. I need to see the Crestmans."

"Crestmans." The man started to scroll down the computer screen and then stopped. "Your name, please?"

"My name? Do you have to—"

"I'll need to tell them your name and ask if they're expecting you."

"Oh, I didn't know...," Hallie began uneasily, and then, getting control of herself, she went on,

"Tell them Hallie. That's H-A-L-L-I-E. Ask for Zachary and tell him Hallie is here to see him."

Mistake! A voice in her head was shouting. *If something terrible has happened you don't want your name mixed up in it. Mistake! Mistake!*

Hallie was still trying to argue with the voice in her head when another one interrupted. "They don't answer," the doorman's voice was saying. "The Crestmans aren't answering and their machine isn't on. They must not be at home."

Hallie stared at the guard indignantly. *They* are *home,* she wanted to shout. *I saw them just a few minutes ago.* But of course she mustn't say that. Anything but that. "But they *are* home," she said. "I know they're home." The guard was staring at her, his eyes asking questions she knew she couldn't answer.

"What do they look like?" he asked.

"Don't you know?" Hallie was amazed and unbelieving.

"No." The guard was smiling. "I've just started here. I haven't gotten to know—"

"Oh, okay. Okay. Maybe they're not home. I'll come back later," she babbled as she backed toward the door.

Outside on the sidewalk she started to run again—and then stopped. Where was she going? Not to look for someone who could tell her what to do. There wasn't anyone. There wasn't anyone who would understand if she said she had been watching this family in their own living room and something bad was happening to them, or was about to happen.

No. No one could help her. She would have to decide what to do all by herself. She must have covered the short distance between the entrance to the mall and the Warwick Mansion in a kind of trance, and then, still lost in thought, sat down on the mansion's front steps. She didn't remember deciding to do it but that was where she still was a few minutes later when a familiar voice said, "Hallie. What are you doing? Did you lose your key?"

"Oh, hi," Hallie said. "Hi, Mom. No, I have my key. I was just—sitting here."

Carrying two bags of groceries, Mom came up a couple of steps and sat down beside her. She looked over at Hallie once or twice, but for quite a while she didn't say anything. Hallie didn't either, but she wished she could. She wished she could tell her mother what she had seen and what she was worrying about. . . . But there just wasn't any way.

Where would she start? With that day in September when she was looking for place to hide and somehow wound up in the forbidden attic? And if she started there, she would have to go on and try to explain the blue-glass spyhole and everything she'd seen through it, right up until today. Right up to what she'd seen happening, or about to happen, to the Crestman family less than an hour ago. No. There was no way.

After a while they both got up. Hallie took one of

160

the bags from her mom and they went on up the stairs together.

That night Hallie managed to put the Crestmans out of her mind. At least she tried hard to, and most of the time she was pretty successful. While she helped get dinner ready and then ate it, she managed to concentrate on what was being said. They talked about the new general manager at the savings and loan and the latest news about Erin and Jolene and the Jason Johnson fan club. And about how Katlyn had asked her if she could come over sometime to help her figure out how to play her new computer game.

But later, in her own room, it was impossible to keep from going back over everything she had seen through the spyhole. Not just that afternoon but every time she'd been there and everything she'd seen and heard about the Crestmans. All of it kept playing through her mind like the rerun of a television story that never got to any sort of ending. At least not to the kind of ending that might help her understand what she'd seen happening that afternoon.

Had there really been a gun in the sideboard drawer? And why had Zachary waved it over his head as he rushed back to where his father was sitting? Could it all be related, in some way, to whatever it was that had been in the newspaper? And what about that time when the poor little kid had been spying on that scary, angry argument from behind the sofa? What had been going on then?

But most of all, Hallie's mind kept going back to whatever it was that Zachary's father and then Zachary himself had taken out of that drawer. Had it really been a gun? Over and over again she closed her eyes and tried to picture it, but the image kept changing and blurring. Sometimes it looked exactly like a gun—but other times she wasn't sure.

Was it or wasn't it? If only she knew even that much for sure, she would know what had to be done. If it wasn't a gun, all she had to do was forget it. But if it was, she really should do something she hated even to think about. What she would have to do was tell her mother first and then probably the police. And part of the telling would have to be about the blue-glass spyhole, and what she, herself, had been doing there ever since the first week in September. For a whole lot of reasons, confessing seemed almost impossible.

But before she decided she had to be absolutely sure. And the only way that might happen was for her to keep looking for Zachary at the library as well as through the spyhole.

Zachary didn't come to the library on Friday, and because she waited there for him for such a long time, she had very little time left to watch for him to show up in the Crestman apartment. And of course he wasn't there either. Nobody was.

As soon as Hallie sat down on the trunk and

leaned forward to the spyhole she saw that the familiar blue-tinged room was empty. But she had been at the window for perhaps a minute before she began to notice that it was even emptier than usual. The longer she stared through the flawed blue glass, the more she began to suspect that, whatever else might have happened to the Crestmans, they were no longer living in the spyhole apartment.

She didn't want to believe it. After all, she told herself, it didn't look all that different. Most of the large, shapeless pieces of furniture were still where they had always been, and there never had been a whole lot more. But now even that little bit was missing. There were no magazines or newspapers on the end tables now, no dishes behind the glass doors of the sideboard, and, most importantly, no fanged and feathered witch-doctor mask on the mantelpiece. The dreary, lifeless spyhole apartment was completely deserted.

Stunned, Hallie went on sitting on the old trunk for an uncertain amount of time trying to guess what might have happened. To figure out why the Crestmans had gone, and most of all, why their disappearance was making her feel so lost and miserable. When she finally got up, crossed the attic, and trudged down the stairs, she still didn't have any answers.

24

So that was that, Hallie thought. The Crestman story was over, and it looked as if she would never know how it ended. For a week or two she thought about it a lot. Every night she went through *The Irvington Times* very carefully, at least the pages that had local stuff like fires and accidents and neighborhood feuds, looking for any mention of the Crestman name, but without any luck. And once or twice a week she made a quick trip to the attic to see if anything had changed in the apartment, but nothing ever had. No sign of the Crestmans, and nothing new that would mean that a different family was moving in.

As time went by she found that she wasn't thinking about the Crestmans as much, but now and then she still wondered whether the beautiful Rapunzel/Tiffany ever got to see her boyfriend, Tony, again. And whether funny little Zachary was still studying about psychiatry and pretending to be a witch doctor.

Now and then she seriously considered telling her mother about the Crestmans. She really wished she could get Mom's opinion on whether or not she should have done something more drastic when she'd seen that gun just before the Crestmans disappeared. Whether she should have called 911 or even the police. But there were other times when she was sure that all Mom would do was freak out over the fact that Hallie had spent all that time in the attic when she knew what might have happened if Mrs. Crowley found out about it. And it really did seem as if it would be too bad to dump the attic problem on Mom right now, just when she was painting again and beginning to seem more like her old self.

After a while Hallie even began to think about the possibility of telling Katlyn a little bit about the Crestmans. Not mentioning the spyhole, of course, just making it into a kind of story. Katlyn loved sad, romantic stuff almost as much as Marty used to. Hallie had found that out when she'd mentioned that her dad had been in the big freeway accident, and something about Katlyn's reaction made her go on talking—and on and on and on. Right while she was babbling away, Hallie had been sure she would be sorry afterward, but for some reason she wasn't.

Hallie was sure the Crestmans would be another story that Katlyn would really get into. She hadn't decided just how much to tell, but she had begun to seriously consider how to bring the subject up the next time she went to Katlyn's house to do homework and play computer games.

On a Saturday morning almost a month after the Crestmans disappeared, Katlyn called and asked Hallie to meet her at Weatherby Park to go skating instead of coming to her house. Hallie's mom was going to be at an art gallery most of the day, so it would be good to have someplace to go, but Hallie was surprised and a little bit disappointed about the park idea. She really liked Katlyn's parents and their house, a big old Victorian with a large yard and all kinds of pets. Being at the McKnights' was a little bit like being back in Bloomfield.

"How come skating, all of a sudden?" she asked.

"Oh, I don't know," Katlyn said. "It's just such a nice day and you said you used to like skating before . . . before you moved to Irvington." She paused for a moment before she went on to ask in a sympathetic tone of voice, "You still have skates, don't you?"

Katlyn had this thing about how poor Hallie and her mother were nowadays. She liked to ask about it, and the weird thing was that Hallie didn't mind answering. She didn't know why, except that you could tell that Katlyn wasn't gloating or even feeling sorry for you when she asked that kind of thing. It was more as if she kind of admired Hallie, envied her almost, for having such an excitingly miserable life. She even liked visiting Hallie at the cell block, where she really got into pretending she was one of the poor maidservants who used to live there.

"Just imagine what it was like for them," Katlyn would say. "Having to work hard all day scrubbing floors and waiting on people, and having no place to call their own except one little dark room." That was Katlyn McKnight for you; she just couldn't help enjoying a good tragedy.

But this time Hallie didn't have any tearjerker story to share with her, since she still had her old in-line skates and they still fit pretty well. "Yeah, I still have them," she said. "Where do you want to meet? At your house?"

"At the park," Katlyn said. "Right there by the duck pond. You remember how to get to the pond?"

Weatherby Park was in the really nice part of Irvington, a long way from Warwick Avenue but not too far from Katlyn's house. If you stayed on the number four bus that went past the McKnights' you went right on up to the park. "Sure," Hallie said. "I remember."

So that was how it happened that Hallie Meredith was walking up the path to the Weatherby Park duck pond at ten o'clock on a Saturday morning, carrying her skates by their long laces over one shoulder and a backpack over the other.

She was almost to the first duck-watching bench when a familiar, high-pitched voice said, "Hey, Hallie. Hallie Meredith." And there above the path, sitting cross-legged on a big flat rock, was Zachary Crestman. Hallie couldn't believe it. What she especially couldn't believe was how glad she was to see him.

"Wow," she said, kind of brain-dead with surprise. "Wow. How did you get here?"

Zachary slid down off the rock and turned around to reach back up for his backpack. Then he bounced down the slope to the path and said, "I walked. How did you get here?"

Hallie stared at him. There he was, looking pretty much like always, the same sharp-edged face, laser-beam brown eyes, and round, fuzzy head. She surprised herself and him too by grabbing his shoulders and giving him a shake that was almost a hug. When that was over she just went on standing there grinning at him. After a while he grinned back briefly before he repeated, "How did you get here?"

"Wow," Hallie said. "You really want to know how I got here, don't you? Okay. I flew, maybe, or . . ." She held up her skates. "Or skated. Yeah, maybe I skated all the way from Warwick Avenue." He just went on staring at her, waiting. When Zachary Crestman asked a question he wanted a straight answer.

"Okay, the truth," Hallie said. "On the bus. And you really walked? Where from? Where do you live now?"

Zachary pointed back toward the entrance to the park. "That way," he said. "Up there at our house on Alderman." His grin got wider. "We live at home now. All of us."

"At home?"

He nodded. "Where we used to live before my mom and dad started getting divorced. Only they've stopped now."

"Stopped what?" Hallie didn't get it.

"Divorcing." Zachary sounded impatient, as if he couldn't see why Hallie was looking so puzzled. "Dad's lawyer got . . ." He stopped and looked around at the people who were walking past them on both sides. The path was getting crowded. "Come on," he said, lowering his voice. "Let's go back up on my rock."

After they'd climbed up the slope and onto the rocky ledge, Zachary went on with what he was saying. "My dad's lawyer retired and Mom's . . ." He stopped to look at Hallie. "You know, the one my dad hit that time when they wrote about us in the paper?"

Hallie nodded and he went on, "Okay. That lawyer moved to Australia, so the divorce kind of just—stopped happening."

"Hey, that's great," Hallie said. So that was what had been going on. Zachary's father had been living in the Towers apartment because he was getting a divorce and Zachary and his sister were . . . "I get it," she said. "That's why you weren't there very much. Sometimes you lived with your mother, right?"

"Yes, sometimes I lived at home with my mother." Zachary's eyes had a faraway look and he was sounding preoccupied, and Hallie found herself staring off into space too. She didn't know what Zachary was thinking about, but what she was thinking was what a lot of time she'd wasted worrying about the whole bunch of them. So there really hadn't been any murder, and if Zachary's father was kind of hard to get along with at times it was probably because he was unhappy about the divorce. There hadn't been any reason to worry at all, except . . . What about the gun?

"But what about the gun?" she asked Zachary.

"What gun?"

"You know, I asked you if there was a gun at your house and you said—"

"There wasn't one," Zachary said. "I told you there wasn't one."

"Yeah, you did," Hallie said. "Okay. But what . . ." She grabbed Zachary's shoulder and turned him around to face her. "Listen," she said. "What was it your dad kept in a big drawer in the dining room sideboard? You know, in his apartment."

"A big drawer?" Zachary asked. "In the dining room?"

Hallie nodded and for a long time Zachary nodded

too, before he said, "Papers I think, and pens. Things like that except . . ." His face suddenly lit up. "Except on my birthday. On my birthday he hid my present in that drawer."

"Oh yeah?" Hallie asked. "When was that?"

"Last month," Zachary said. He grinned suddenly. "The same day that we all went back home. Right after Dad gave me my present my mom called up and said for us to come over. All of us. My dad too. So we did and the next day we all moved back home."

Hallie was beginning to get the picture. Zachary's dad had been sitting there in his big chair and Zachary came in looking nervous, as if maybe he was wondering if his dad had forgotten his birthday, only he was sort of afraid to ask and then . . .

"Hey," Hallie had a sudden brainstorm. "I'll bet I know what your dad gave you. I'll bet it was a toy gun. Was it?"

Zachary stared at her. "No!" he said, sounding shocked and angry. "Why would he do that? A nine-year-old person doesn't play with toy guns."

Hallie had never seen him so indignant, not even when he thought she'd pushed him down on the sidewalk. "Well, all right. All right. I was just asking. So what did he give you?"

It took Zachary a minute or two to calm down enough to pay attention to the question. But when he did his grin came back. Definitely a nine-year-old grin, wide and uncomplicated. "He gave me just what

I always wanted ever since I was a little kid. He gave—"
He stopped suddenly, and grabbing his backpack, he
opened it and started taking things out. A couple of
books, a notebook, a pair of binoculars, and then
something black and chunky. At one end there was a
tiny keyboard and monitor screen. "He gave me this,"
he said triumphantly. "An electronic notebook."

Hallie stared at the little computer. "Here," she
said. "Let me see." Taking it out of Zachary's hands,
she held it in her own, turning it this way and that
and covering one end of it with her fingers. "Yes,
maybe," she murmured. When one end of the electronic notebook was covered, the other end sticking
out of her fist did look a little like the handgrip of a
pistol. At least it did if you were kind of expecting
it to.

"That gun stuff," Zachary said. "I bet you
dreamed it."

"Yeah," Hallie said. "I guess I did."

25

That Saturday in Weatherby Park turned out to be full of surprises. Running into Zachary and then finding out that there hadn't ever been a gun in the sideboard drawer was the first big surprise, but it wasn't the only one. Hallie was still sitting right there on the rocky ledge above the duck pond, learning how to use Zachary's electronic notebook, when he suddenly flopped over on his side and pulled his empty backpack over his head.

"What is it?" Hallie demanded, trying to pull the backpack off his head. "What's the matter with you?"

"Down there on the path. Look!" Zachary's voice sifting out through the canvas had a muffled sound.

"Look at what?" All she could see was a mother with a kid in a stroller, and behind her some teenagers. A tall, broad-shouldered teenage guy walking along with . . . wow. The girl was . . . "It's Rapun— I mean, Tiffany." She poked Zachary again. "It's your sister, isn't it?" she said.

Zachary pulled the backpack tighter over his face. "I know, I know," he was whispering. "Keep still. Don't talk to me. Don't let her see me."

Hallie was bewildered, but she quit poking Zachary and trying to talk to him. Instead she concentrated on noticing how the beautiful Tiffany looked up at her handsome boyfriend and fluttered her long dark eyelashes. And then as they walked on past how her hair gleamed in the sunlight as it slid across her shoulders and drifted on down below her waist in a sleek, shimmery curtain.

It wasn't until Hallie whispered, "Okay. They're gone," that Zachary sat up and took the backpack off his head.

"Hey." Something had just occurred to Hallie. "I thought you said Tiffany's boyfriend had a ring in his nose. I didn't see any ring."

"I know," Zachary said. "He doesn't have one. The one with the nose ring was Tony. This one is Gary. He plays football. My dad likes this one okay."

Hallie had to think about that for a minute before she asked, "Why were you hiding? Why didn't you want them to see you?"

Zachary looked embarrassed. He put his books back into his backpack and started fiddling with its Velcro flaps before he answered, "Because she's mean. Tiffany is. If she sees me when she's with any of her boyfriends she always says I'm spying on her, even when I'm not. Like now, for instance. Then she slugs me." Before he went on Zachary rubbed his jaw as if he was remembering a recent slug. "Tiffany is a very good slugger."

"Can't you tell your parents?" Hallie asked. "Won't they make her knock it off?"

Still rubbing his jaw, Zachary grinned. "You mean my head?"

Hallie grinned back. "No, you idiot. I meant can't they make her stop slugging you?"

Zachary's smile vanished suddenly. "No. I can't do that because—" He sighed deeply. "I can't because I'm afraid they'll fight about it."

"Who'll fight?"

"My parents. My mother says it's Tiffany's fault and my dad says it's mine. Then they fight about it."

That was a real downer. She couldn't help feeling bad about poor little Zachary having to worry all the time about giving his parents something to fight about. A hand reached out and almost patted him on his fuzzy head before Hallie realized it was hers. She jerked it back then and put it behind her, feeling sure he would resent it.

The whole thing about Tiffany's boyfriend was kind of depressing too. Right at first Hallie didn't know why, but after she thought for a while she said, "But Tiffany cried about Tony. Her eyes were all red and there were dark smudges around her eyes. Like bruises."

Zachary stared at her. "How did you...," he

started, but then he nodded and said in a very suspicious voice, "I know. In your dreams." After a minute he shrugged and said, "Tiffany cries a lot."

"And the bruises?"

He shook his head. "No," he said. "I don't think so. Mascara, I think. It happens when she cries."

Hallie was amazed and confused. There was so much to think about, but before she could even really begin she heard someone calling her name. This time the caller was Katlyn. Hallie jumped off the ledge and slid down the slope to meet her.

Katlyn looked a little bit angry. "What were you doing up there?" she asked. "Didn't you see me? I've skated past here twice looking for you."

"I'm sorry," Hallie said. "I was just really busy talking to . . ." She pointed up to where Zachary was still sitting. "To this little kid I used to know." She gave Katlyn one of her best unstarching smiles, and it kind of worked. Katlyn's frown had started to disappear when Zachary skidded down the slope and bumped into her. Katlyn skated backward and then forward trying not to fall down and when she finally got her balance again she stared at nerdy little Zachary and then at Hallie with an "I don't believe it" look on her face.

Hallie tried to make her own smile say "Yeah I know" and also "I'll explain later." Then she said, "Look, Zachary. Let me see that computer notebook for a minute." Zachary fished it out of his backpack and Hallie punched in her phone number and the words CALL ME MONDAY. RIGHT AFTER SCHOOL.

When she handed it back to Zachary he read it and grinned. "Okay," he said. "I need to find out about..." He looked at Katlyn and his voice dwindled away.

"About...?" Hallie prompted him.

He looked at Katlyn again before he punched something into his computer and held it out for Hallie to see. YOUR DREAMS it said on the little screen. Standing on tiptoe, he whispered in Hallie's ear, "I still don't believe it." Then he bounced off down the path.

The rest of the day Hallie and Katlyn skated and ate lunch, and Hallie told Katlyn a lot about Zachary's sad story. She didn't mention the spyhole, though. Without actually saying so, she made it sound as if she'd just met Zachary at the library and he'd started telling her about his problems. All about his beautiful, mean sister and his father who was mean too, at least when he was feeling angry about the divorce that he and his wife were getting. And how they were back together now, and maybe it would stay that way and maybe it wouldn't.

And that brought up how Mr. Crestman had punched his wife's lawyer and Zachary was so embarrassed by the story that was in the paper that it made him cry. It was Katlyn's kind of story and before Hallie was through she could tell that Katlyn was hooked.

"The poor kid," she kept saying. "That's so sad. It's such a sad story. Such a little kid having so much to worry about. We ought to do something about it. Don't you think?"

Hallie couldn't help grinning, at least inwardly. That was Katlyn for you. Not that she was perfect. She could be moody sometimes and even kind of bad tempered, but it was just that she was really interested in other people. All kinds of people.

"Sure," Hallie said. "Let's do something."

26

Hallie had a lot to think about on the way home that afternoon. Most of the time she thought about the fascinating stuff she'd learned about the Crestmans. Especially about the gun she'd been so worried about that had really been a palm-sized computer. And how the Tony/Tiffany tragedy turned out to be not so tragic after all. Which, to Hallie's surprise, was actually kind of disappointing. She wasn't sure why, since she'd always preferred stories with happy endings, and having a new boyfriend that your father didn't hate quite as much seemed like a fairly happy one. At least, happy for Tiffany.

But for Tony? Hallie couldn't help wishing she'd had a chance to see him before he got replaced by the football guy. Just a glimpse, to see if he looked at all like the person she'd been imagining when the beautiful Rapunzel stared out the window, whispering his name and messing up her mascara with tears. Was he, Hallie wondered, tall, dark, and, in spite of the ring in his nose, incredibly handsome, the way she'd imagined him? She really wished she knew.

But mostly she thought about what might happen to Zachary and the rest of his family. Would his parents stay married this time the way Zachary wanted them to? Hallie hoped they would, but remembering how they'd looked at each other that day when Zachary was watching from behind the sofa, she had her doubts. She hated to think what it would do to Zachary if they split up again. Anyway, she was glad she'd given him her phone number so he could let her know what was happening. Like Katlyn said, maybe there was something they could do.

While the crowded bus jiggled and clattered through downtown Irvington, Hallie thought mostly about the Crestmans, but now and then something reminded her that she had a few problems of her own. Like blistered toes, for instance.

She hadn't noticed the pain that much while she was still skating, but she was certainly noticing it now, and she knew exactly what it meant. What it meant was that her expensive in-line skates really were getting to be too small. She was outgrowing them, all right, and she knew her mother wouldn't be able to buy her a new pair anytime soon.

Taking the skates down from where she'd hung them over her shoulder, Hallie put them in her lap and ran her fingers over the nice, soft leather.

They weren't very old, actually. Her father had

bought them for her less than a year ago. And now . . .
The old familiar rush of aching anger was just starting to swell up through her chest and into her throat as the bus lumbered to a stop on Warwick Avenue. Hallie swallowed hard, hung her skates back over her shoulder, shoved her way to the door, and got off. She was still gritting her teeth and blinking back angry tears as she made her way past the video rental and the fast-food restaurant and on to the wide flight of stairs that led up to the front door of Warwick Mansion.

She had started up the cracked marble steps when she glanced up and something caught her eye. Something was moving in the second-floor tower window. Shading her eyes, she looked up and saw it again, a blurry movement behind the green and yellow glass. And then, way up in the clear glass above the decorative panels, a face appeared. It was Mrs. Tilson, looking down at Hallie and waving.

Hallie stared in surprise. To be looking out from way up there above the stained-glass panels, she must be standing on the window seat. Hallie hoped she didn't lose her balance and fall off. She waved back and Mrs. Tilson waved again. Her lips were moving, saying something, but what? Was something wrong? Did the Tilsons need help? Hallie waved again and made her lips form the words "What is it? Is something wrong?" but the only answer was more waving.

Hallie ran then, up the stairs, through the double

doors, and on up to the second-floor hallway. She knocked hard on the Tilsons' front door, waited a moment, and knocked again. When the door finally opened she and Mrs. Tilson started talking at the same time, two people saying in breathless unison, "Is something wrong?"

It was Mrs. Tilson who answered first. "No, nothing's wrong. Why did you . . . ?"

Hallie relaxed. "I was just surprised to see you way up there." She pointed toward the tower room window. "I thought maybe you needed to get someone's attention because . . ."

Mrs. Tilson giggled and then shrugged. "No, no. Nothing's wrong. I was just looking out at the avenue and then suddenly there you were." She shrugged and giggled again. "You know, I told you that I like to—"

Hallie interrupted "—look out of windows," she said. "Yes, I know. You said looking out windows was healthy, or something like that."

"Did I say that?" Mrs. Tilson looked surprised. "Why, yes, I guess I did. I wonder . . ." She stopped and looked Hallie over. "Won't you come on in? Come in and we'll talk about it some more."

"Well." Hallie hesitated. "I'd better go up and put all this stuff away first. Oh, and leave a note for my mom. But maybe I could come back after I do that."

"Oh yes, do," Mrs. Tilson said. "Please do."

Back in the cell block Hallie wrote a note and left it on the kitchen table before she went to her room. She threw her backpack on the bed and was squeezing around the bed to put the skates in the closet when she found herself face to face with the oval mirror. She stopped to stare at herself for a moment. At the dark, slanted eyebrows above the wide-set eyes and high cheekbones. And at the spot on her right cheek where she could make a dimple appear—when she felt like it. Most of the time lately she'd felt more like ... Narrowing her eyes in a ferocious glare, she raised the left side of her upper lip the way Zeus used to do when he was mad at another dog. She stared at her snarling face for a few seconds before she sat down on the bed and began to think.

Could looking out a window really be good for you? In her own case, had the spyhole window been good for her? In one way, it had only given her a lot more stuff to worry about. But in another way—she didn't like to admit it, probably wouldn't admit it if anyone should ask, but things in her life had been getting better since she'd started looking out of that particular window.

No, maybe not. Not *getting* better so much as *feeling* better. Things were pretty much the same in her life. Maybe the change was in how she felt about it. Tipping over backward on the bed, Hallie frowned up at the cracked ceiling and imagined herself saying to Mrs. Tilson or to anyone else who might want to know, "But that doesn't mean I'm back to okay. Not if okay means the way I was before. There's no way looking out a window, even a thousand windows, could make things the way they were before."

There was a humming noise first. A pulsing, humming sound that seemed to fill her whole head and make a throbbing beat in her ears. Her eyelids fluttered heavily. She rolled her head back and forth but her eyes refused to stay open and the humming sound didn't go away. Instead it blurred and deepened and turned into words. It said her name first. "Hallie," it said, and then, "Windows, Hallie. Look for the windows."

The voice was so loud and real that suddenly she was wide awake and sitting bolt upright. "Wh-what...," she stammered. "Who? Who said that?"

But the answer, if there was going to be one, was drowned out by the sharp click of a key turning in a lock, the thump of a door swinging open against the wall, and then a series of familiar footsteps going toward the kitchen. Mom was home. Still startled and confused, Hallie got up off the bed and followed her mother down the hall.

Mom was bending over the refrigerator's vegetable bin when Hallie said hi, and she straightened up quickly with a bunch of carrots in her hand. "Oh, hello," she gasped. "You startled me. I didn't hear you come in." But then her smile faded. "What is it, Hallie? Is something wrong?"

"No, not really. It's just that..." Hallie paused, shaking her head. "I guess maybe I was dreaming but I just heard this voice talking to me. I was lying on my bed and then I heard someone talking to me, and it kind of scared me."

Mom put down the carrots and led Hallie to a chair and sat down beside her. "Tell me," she said. "Tell me about it. What did the voice say?"

"It said my name and then it said something about windows."

Mom looked puzzled. "Windows? I don't see what..."

"Yeah." Hallie grinned ruefully. "It doesn't make much sense. But it's kind of like something Mrs. Tilson says. About windows and mirrors."

"Really? Mrs. Tilson? Windows and mirrors?"

Hallie nodded. "It's something she likes to talk about. About how looking out windows is a lot better for a person than looking in mirrors. Or something like that."

Mom shook her head. "I'm afraid I don't understand," she said.

"I know. I don't either. Except..." Suddenly, without even figuring it out beforehand, Hallie began to explain. "Except that mirrors are just for looking at yourself and windows are for looking at other people."

"Well, that's true as far as—" Mom was starting to say when Hallie interrupted.

"Oh, I almost forgot. I have to go." She pulled her scribbled note out from under one of the grocery bags and shoved it into Mom's hand.

" 'At Tilsons'. Back soon. Hallie,' " Mom read out loud.

"Right," Hallie said. "I saw Mrs. Tilson on my way up and she asked me to come down for a visit."

"Oh, good." Mom was fishing in one of the bags. "There's something here you can take her."

Hallie grinned. "Let me guess," she said.

Mom nodded. "Right," she said, holding out a carton of yogurt. "And while you're there ask her to explain some more about the windows thing. Tell her I'm very interested."

A minute later Hallie was on her way down the hall, carrying a quart of vanilla yogurt. As she passed her room she stepped inside for a second.

"Well, I understand," she whispered. "I do understand about the windows thing, now. But what I don't understand is why You bothered to mention it. I thought we still weren't speaking."

She went on then, out the door and down the hall, still thinking about windows. About the secret spy-hole window, and all the other windows she might someday find ways to look through.